Vodka & Chocolate Drops

VODKA AND CHOCOLATE DROPS

A BLUEBERRY SPRINGS SWEET ROMANCE

JEAN ORAM

Vodka and Chocolate Drops
A Blueberry Springs Sweet Romance (Book 5) © 2015 Jean Oram

Printed in the United States of America unless otherwise stated on the last page of this book. Published by Oram Productions Alberta, Canada.

Cover design by Najla Qamber Designs and Media

Complete cataloguing information available online or upon request.
Oram, Jean.
Vodka and Chocolate Drops: A Blueberry Springs Sweet Romance / Jean Oram.—1st. ed.
ISBN 978-1-928198-99-4, 978-1-928198-78-9, 978-1-928198-21-5 (paperback)
Ebook ISBN 978-1-928198-20-8
Summary: On the path to true love with her best friend, Amber unearths devastating family secrets which not only change who she believes she is, but changes the small town of Blueberry Springs as well.
First Oram Productions Edition: September 2019

ACKNOWLEDGMENTS

I would like to thank Kate and Clare at CLIC Sargent for helping families with cancer in the UK and for organizing the Get in Character auction. It's not an easy job wrangling authors or auctioning off spots for winners to be named in upcoming novels. *Vodka and Chocolate Drops* was one of the honored titles included in the 2015 auction and its winners were Steven and Emma Lunt. One-hundred percent of their donation went to CLIC Sargent and will help families who have children with cancer. Thank you! The character Steven and Emma asked to be included in the novel was their unborn baby girl, Blossom Lunt. May Blossom be healthy, happy, and fill your hearts with love and laughter.

A special thank you also goes to the team who helped keep this story on track; Lucy Marsden, Margaret Carney, Emily Kirkpatrick, and Erin Dixon. As well, a big thank you to my fans. I definitely couldn't continue to do this without you. I hope you enjoy *Vodka and Chocolate Drops* as much as my other Blueberry Springs novels.

1

Don't watch their special guest, Amber. Turn off the TV.

Amber Thompson cranked up the show's volume and perched on the arm of the couch, her breathing becoming unsteady as she waited for her ex-boyfriend to take to the screen. With trembling hands she checked to see if the tub of double chocolate ice cream was really and truly empty. It was.

That was the thing about breakups. They made you desperate to fill the gaping hole inside, desperate to avoid the evil, heartbreaking ex forever, and yet still starved for every detail about him.

Amber sighed and went for the dill pickle chips, mowing her way through the mess of crumbs in the bag's bottom as the man she'd lived with for the past year appeared before her in his new role as a debut novelist--smiling, confident, charming. Everything.

It was his time to shine.

Her chest tightened and she riffled through a bowl of discarded foil wrappers from chocolate drops. She'd been such a fool. How had she ever convinced herself that a handsome, award-winning newscaster would stay with her forever? She should have known that he wouldn't choose permanence with her, a small mountain-town nobody.

A choking feeling welled up inside her as Russell Peaks was introduced by the show's host. The suit she'd helped Russell choose hung beautifully off his trim shoulders. He looked happy and relaxed. Not at all like someone who had just ditched his live-in girlfriend by phone the night before.

He'd delivered the lines she'd been half expecting since their first kiss: *Amber, babe, I can't do this back-and-forth thing between the city and Blueberry Springs anymore. It's over. I won't be coming back.*

Other than to collect his belongings from their shared rental and tow away the holiday trailer he used as a writing cave, of course. Stuff she planned to have ready at the end of the property by the time he came for it tonight.

She didn't want to face him and the fact that she wasn't enough, wasn't special enough. She was just a nobody who had gone to the city in hopes of finding whatever was unique inside herself, and instead she'd found someone to use her. She'd spent months coaxing Russell through writer's block and periods of self-doubt, and now that his life, his world, was taking off he'd dismissed and rejected her, just as her father had before she was even born.

Her life was never going to change. She was never going to be anyone special.

The interviewer asked Russell, "What was your inspiration for *Ember Unfolded*?"

"I've always been crazy enough to believe I can change the world with the written word, whether as a newscaster, reporter, or novelist," Amber whispered, expecting him to say the lines he'd rehearsed in front of their bedroom mirror.

But instead of his practiced lines, Russell said, "Inspiration was all around me as I wrote this book."

The only thing that had been all around him was Amber, and she was hardly inspiring. What a big fat liar he was.

She found a chocolate drop and popped it in her mouth, disappointed that it didn't seem to help her mood.

"Rumor has it you're dating a woman named Amber. It's not a difficult leap to assume that *Ember Unfolded's* main character, Ember, may have been based on her."

Amber sat straighter. She'd been mentioned on air.

The interviewer thought Amber was the main character.

Her skin ran cold, then hot, and she almost lost the chocolate drop when her mouth fell open.

She'd begged Russell for months to let her read the manuscript, but he'd insisted it was a surprise. She'd felt frustrated, yet special at the time, but now she wasn't sure the book was going to be the type of surprise she would appreciate.

She scrambled up the creaking wooden staircase to the bedroom, then pawed through the drawers of Russell's bedside table, looking for the key to his mobile writing office, where he kept copies of the manuscript. Nothing. All the drawers were surprisingly empty. She ran to the bureau where he kept his clothes. Also empty. He'd been moving out for weeks and she hadn't noticed. He'd been using her right up until the final hour before his success, then had discarded her like garbage.

She took in their bedroom with fresh eyes. A *Writer's Digest* and *Newsweek* on the nightstand, a stack of books on the bureau and a print he'd chosen on the wall. That was it. The only signs that he'd slept in this room for a year.

Below, Amber could hear Russell on TV. "That's the mystery, isn't it? Who is Ember?" There was a pause, then in a quieter, not quite reverent tone, he said, "Amber Thompson and I are no longer dating."

Ember Unfolded. The title had never made any sense to her, but now... Ember was the heroine and inspiration had been all around him.

If he'd dumped her on the eve of his book's release, "Ember" couldn't be good news.

Swallowing the panic that was ripping away her strength, Amber ran down the stairs two at a time, avoiding the one at the bottom with the loose board. She rummaged through the junk-food wrappers on the coffee table, looking for her car keys. She needed to read the book. She needed to know the truth.

Now.

The interviewer was still asking about the Ember/Amber connection, and Russell replied quickly, "She hasn't read the book. And no, it has nothing to do with our breakup."

Amber froze, fingers of dreading clawing their way up her spine.

She began digging faster for her keys.

Russell had not only used her, but had lied to her by omitting what the book was truly about.

Her tablet. She could get the book without even leaving the house. She flicked through apps until she found the one she wanted, then bought and downloaded Russell's book, livid that she had to pay for a book she had helped create--both advertently and inadvertently. She glanced up at the TV in time to see a woman join Russell on the studio couch. His editor, Sabrina. She was gorgeous and everything Amber wasn't. Her glossy hair a rippling sheen over her super-toned shoulders. Her black dress hugging every slim curve of her well-defined body. She had impossible hips and no apparent belly roll. How could a woman even survive with that little body fat?

Russell gave Sabrina a long kiss on the lips and Amber stood suddenly, knocking over the coffee table, sending her tablet flying. Her ex broke the kiss and smiled at the camera again.

Smiled at Amber.

That son of a...

Everything suddenly became clear.

Stress hadn't caused Russell to become more and more distant over the past few months.

The workload as a debut author and the long drive from the city hadn't led to the late nights.

The book's problematic pacing wasn't responsible for the distracted look in his eyes.

And the nights when he never came home? Those weren't caused by late-day business meetings. It was because of Sabrina. All of it Sabrina.

Amber had played the fool and now everyone she knew would see it. Everyone would know how blind and naive she'd been. It was all right there in high definition. She fell onto the couch, gripping her head, trying to hold everything in, trying to stop the desperate thoughts slamming through her mind.

She made herself focus on Sabrina's perfectly made up lips. Lips that had just kissed Russell. Had kissed him before. Casually. Passionately. Lips that claimed ownership. Lips that had probably kissed him while... *no, don't think about it.*

Amber bunched her hands into fists, while her heart pounded hard and fast. He had been hers, the only thing keeping her from a life as a small-town nothing. And he'd used her. Lied to her. Cheated on her.

"Now Russell, don't be so mysterious," Sabrina teased, her voice laced with a flirtatious note that made Amber want to barf. "You can tell them about your muse."

When he remained silent, the interviewer asked him how much artistic license he'd taken and whether Ember was real.

Sabrina laughed in a way that made it clear she had plenty to say on the subject. "Russell was very fortunate in that--"

"A gentleman never kisses and tells," he interrupted.

Amber grabbed the tablet, her mind barely functioning as she skimmed the first chapter. She set down the book, unable to take any more. What she'd read proved he was a liar. He'd kissed. He'd told. It didn't matter what coy lines he used on television, it was all there in the opening text. He'd taken something intimate and sacred. He'd taken her trust and betrayed her.

The sounds in the room narrowed until the only thing Amber could hear was her own heartbeat, the force of its thumping breaking her, little by little.

The program changed from the noon show to a soap opera, and its theme song woke Amber from her shock.

How had she been so desperate for love and recognition that she'd become blind to what Russell was really doing, to who he really was?

Who would be that dumb?

A nobody. A stupid, desperate, needy loser trying to live in a world where she obviously had never belonged.

Tears slipped down her cheeks as she stood. She couldn't stay here any longer, surrounded by memories of Russell. She needed to leave before everyone in Blueberry Springs got hold of this and she became the talk of the town. After running upstairs, she began tossing her clothes and toiletries into a duffel bag, then hurried on through the old house, collecting her computer and other possessions. Ten minutes later, she dropped the bag in her car and slammed its protesting door as she turned to stare at the place.

If she ran away she would be letting Russell win one more time. She'd be making it easy for him to collect his last few things and skip off into his future of fortune and fame. By running, she'd be telling everyone in her hometown that Russell was right: she was a nobody anyone could use, and it was easy--she'd just disappear.

And if she left, she would be leaving her mother to deal with the ensuing gossip about her only daughter. Her mom would be left to defend Amber and all her failings. Alone.

Determined, Amber marched back into the house and began collecting items Russell had left behind or brought into their home. Picture frames, throw pillows, a vase, books, music, dishes, collectibles, magazines—everything she could get her hands on. Unable to carry more and unable to find a cardboard box, she stormed outside, where she opened her arms, satisfied with how things crashed and smashed at her feet as they tumbled down the front steps. Ignoring the gorgeous mountain view, she turned and entered the house once again. Room by room she cleared everything of Russell, wishing it felt more cathartic. But the more she worked, the more her mind replayed the hurt of how he'd used her, lied to her, then made it all public.

With tears streaking her cheeks, she ripped at the bed. After balling the linens in her arms, she opened the window and whipped them out into the early spring chill. The mattress! She wanted to burn the mattress. She wanted to burn the whole place down so there would be nothing left for Russell to face but her and the effects of his betrayal.

Anger roared through her veins with a power that made her arms shake and her quads throb as she thought again about the way he'd kept the book a secret from her. How she'd brought him meals in his little holiday trailer. How she'd been so excited to be a part of his world and to be living with a writer.

Hide-a-key. He'd hidden a key on the outside of the trailer. Within minutes she'd found its hiding spot on the RV's underside, and popped the door, dumping all his possessions inside. Next, she went to the machinery shed where Russell's aunt--their landlord--stored her late husband's old backhoe and bulldozer. Amber couldn't tow the trailer out of the yard with her car, but with the backhoe she could.

She started up the machine and then, after experimenting with the levers and pedals, eased it out into the uneven, sloping yard, lifting the tongue of Russell's trailer with the bucket. She began tentatively backing the trailer around the house, planning to leave it parked along the property's edge. If she didn't have to talk to her ex again she'd be less likely to say something that would result in a sequel to *Ember Unfolded*. Or end up sued for placing her foot so far up his you-know-what that he'd need dentures.

She turned the backhoe's bucket, trying to angle the trailer away from the yard's steep drop-off. She could easily end up with it pinned against the cliff's edge if she wasn't careful. But instead of turning away from the dry gulch, it veered closer. Amber slammed on the brakes before the RV went too far, but the sudden stop popped the trailer's tongue off the bucket, and she watched, aghast, as Russell's writing cave bounced along the ground, away from her. She let out a squeak as it rolled over the edge, disappearing as though it had been pulled by an undertow.

She jumped out of the machine and peered over the cliff. The trailer struck the rocky bottom as she watched, its thin walls shattering on impact, sending up a cloud of papers as its propane tank exploded, engulfing the debris in a massive ball of flame.

Well then.

With jellylike legs she patted the air beside her, seeking something to support her. This was definitely going to complicate things.

AMBER SAT on an outcropping of rocks, watching the flames consume what had been her ex-boyfriend's writing room. Big clouds of black smoke billowed up from the valley below, sending birds flying in all directions.

Now this was cathartic. She only wished she'd done it intentionally and that Russell had been here to see it all. She wanted him to know what he'd done to her, and to feel remorse-- the kind that would keep him up at night. She wanted him to see what his little game of fame was costing her on a personal level.

In reality, though, she hoped she never saw him again and that the whole world would forget about him and his book. She even dared hope that women who heard her story went out and burned *Ember Unfolded* in an act of woman-scorned solidarity.

As the chill of the rocks beneath her seeped through her jeans, Amber wondered how she had ever managed to fool herself into thinking she loved Russell enough to turn a blind eye to all the little facts about him and his project that had never lined up enough to make her feel truly secure.

A million revenge plots ripped through her mind as she thought of all the ways she'd allowed herself to be deceived. She struggled to focus less on the anger that was making her head hurt and more on calming down.

Take in the mountainous solitude. The birds. The clouds. Breathe in, two, three, four. Breathe out, two, three, four.

What a prick! She couldn't believe he'd done that to her. And so publicly.

Stop it. Stop thinking. Breathe in. Breathe--what a complete fool she was! She hoped there had been some good stuff in the trailer. Stuff he'd actually miss, because he sure as heck wouldn't be missing her now that his book was released. How had she fallen for--no. *Focus on breathing. Breathe in, two, three, four.*

In the distance, fire trucks roared up the gravel road to the old ranch, clouds of dust whirling behind them similar to the smoke still billowing out of the gulch. Amber climbed down the outcropping, wrapping her arms around herself against the cool wind rolling down the mountains. She felt depleted, exhausted, and her mind refused to shut up about Russell and his betrayal.

A police truck pulled up beside her, tires locking, and Amber's best friend, Scott Malone, leaped out, looking so utterly relieved to see her safe that tears sprang to Amber's eyes. Why couldn't she fall for a man like him? Someone who cared deeply and didn't betray her at every turn. Someone who was always there for her no matter what.

She fell into Scott's outstretched arms and he crushed her against him. He smelled of sunshine and Old Spice, and felt like everything good and safe. He released her and held her out in front of him. He was tall, broad, and as handsome as ever in his police uniform. And worried as all get-out.

"Are you okay?" He gave her shoulders a light shake when she didn't reply immediately.

She nodded and he pulled her back into a hug so fierce she could barely draw in a breath without breaking a rib. She tapped his shoulder, an old wrestling move from gym class that told him he needed to ease up. He used to pin her down just for fun and his bulk had always been oddly comforting, but right now it was a bit too much.

He held her in front of him once more giving her another look of assessment before tugging her close again, inhaling as he squeezed.

"I saw Russell on the news," he said, his voice laden with anger. "And then to get the call that there was a possible explosion and fire up here." He finally released her, his jaw clenched so tight Amber was surprised he still had teeth.

"I'm sorry if I scared you," she said, her voice trembling. She wanted to snuggle against him once more, he felt so good, strong, comforting. In his arms she was safe, loved, unjudged.

Firefighters had begun spraying water into the deep gulch, the droplets dispersing before they reached the flames. A few men prepped to rappel closer with hoses, opting to forgo a helicopter.

"What happened?" Scott asked, taking in the scene.

Heat rushed to Amber's cheeks. How could she explain this to Scott, the cool, collected man who always did the right thing, dated the right women--women who went on to become beauty queens or mayors of neighboring towns? How could Amber tell him she'd foolishly trusted the wrong guy, then made a poor move while trying to rid her life of his possessions after he'd revealed the depth of his betrayal on national television?

"Um..."

"Why is there a backhoe?" Scott squeezed his forehead with

his thumb and index finger as though trying to push away a headache. "Please tell me you didn't do any of the things I'm thinking you did."

Amber gave her friend a pleading look. "It was an accident. I swear."

"An accident?"

"Really. You have to believe me. I was mad--so mad, but I didn't mean to do this."

Scott was quiet for a moment, then gave a sharp nod. "I'm going to talk to the firefighters. Stay here."

Amber watched him move, solid and in charge, the firemen turning as one to greet him.

Having the fire team here was definitely not going to help make this whole situation with Russell and his book go away, as she wanted it to. There was going to be even more gossip to deal with once they told the story to the town.

She probably should have run away. She eyed her aging car. Maybe it wasn't too late. It was still packed from earlier.

Scott rejoined her. "They don't think there's a risk of forest fire, but want to spray adjacent areas in case." He crooked his neck so he was eye to eye with her. "You sure you're okay?"

She wrapped her arms around herself and shrugged. Of course she wasn't okay. She was in the news. She'd been exposed as the heroine in a book her ex had written. She'd been deceived. And now she'd destroyed everything her ex had left behind. This wasn't a typical breakup and things could get very messy if insurance didn't cover heavy machinery whoopsies.

"I saw the interview at noon and I know it's hard--"

"That's what she said," Amber said, twisting his innocent words into an innuendo--her fallback reaction when it came to deflecting attention from her frequent shortcomings. The last thing she needed was sympathy from her best friend seeing as his life was essentially the definition of perfect harmony.

Her joke didn't cause Scott to break into his usual smile.

Instead, a fine line formed between his brows. "Are you done making light of this?"

"It was an accident, okay? I slammed on the brakes when it was going too close to the edge, and the trailer's tongue came off the bucket. I couldn't catch it."

Scott studied her for a moment. "Not an accidentally-on-purpose incident?" His own arms were crossed, his eyes boring into her in a way that unnerved her. "Russell wasn't very nice to you on TV. I could see how that might cause a desire for retribution."

Scott was baiting her for a confession. He was questioning her as an officer of the law. How dare he! They were best friends.

"Don't take that insinuating tone with me," she said, poking him in the chest and then regretting it. The man had to be wearing a flak jacket, as she'd just about busted her finger. "You *know* me. I would never intentionally engage in the destruction of another person's property."

"I'm just doing my job. It's nothing personal."

"I don't think you could get less personal."

Scott's jaw flexed, his expression unreadable. "I can't allow my personal bias to interfere with an investigation."

"Investigation!"

"Anytime there's an explosion, the fire department is called and insurance may be involved, I have a duty to check things out."

Scott was so familiar, yet unexpectedly different. He was very much an authoritative man-in-charge instead of her goofy pal who always tried to make her smile. It still surprised her, after being in Blueberry Springs for almost a year, that her best friend was no longer that lanky kid she used to cause mischief with, but was now a respected member of the community, an officer of the law. She usually admired that, but right now she needed her friend.

She sat heavily on one of the boulders that lined the driveway, wishing there was someone who understood.

"Amber," Scott said softly, his jaw working, his brow drawn low, "I have to know that you're done with this stint of revenge. That you won't hurt Russell. That you're safe."

She jumped up, insulted that he would even have to ask--job or not. "You know me better than anyone else does. You *know* I won't go after him and that this was all an accident."

Tears were threatening to spill over once more, so she stopped talking and sat again, facing away from Scott.

"Amber, you've been through a lot today. It's normal to crave payback."

"What I want is for everything to go away."

Sighing, Scott sat beside her, wrapping an arm around her shoulders. She tried to lean away, but ended up giving in, savoring his strength and the way his body felt against hers.

They sat quietly for a few minutes, then Scott said, "It's meat loaf night at Mom and Dad's. You should join us."

Amber had joined them often enough to be considered one of the family, but tonight she needed some space to think--away from Scott and his new investigative side.

"I think I should avoid town for a while."

"The community will side with you--you're one of us."

"I don't want them to side with me, I want them to pretend nothing happened in my life over the past year. That Russell never existed."

The hurt and humiliation at what Russell had done seared through her once again. In a city, something like this was no big deal. It would be in the papers for a day or two, then drift away. But in a town such as Blueberry Springs, the fact that she was in a book would follow her forever. Add in that Russell had kept secrets from her, and she'd destroyed his well-known writing cave in return, and she was going to be the topic of some pretty hot gossip from now until she lucked out and an alien invasion overshadowed her life.

"Amber…" Scott's voice was rough.

"You don't understand." Sudden anger ripped through her. There was no way a man like Scott could ever even begin to understand what she was feeling. "This kind of stuff will never happen to you. You date Wonder Women. You're perfect. Kind."

Scott simply took her hand, leading her toward his truck.

She slipped from his grip, softening the physical rejection by tentatively placing her palm against his chest, stopping him from herding her toward his vehicle. "People expect great things from you, and you pull through every time. You're a perfect catch, Scott. A perfect man for any woman lucky enough to snag your affection. I truly hope you never understand what my day has been like, but don't say you understand or that I'm overreacting."

"Don't be so hard on yourself. Russell wasn't…" She could see Scott fighting with the urge to say something unkind about her ex. "He didn't deserve you. He never did."

Amber swallowed a lump in her throat, which she figured was the last of her pride. "I made myself try when a part of me knew all along that he wasn't the real deal. I blinded myself to what was really going on."

How could she blame Russell for walking all over her when she'd all but put out a welcome mat? She'd known and yet she'd still hoped, like the foolish woman she was.

Scott wrapped his hand around the one she still held against his chest.

She tipped her chin up so tears wouldn't fall, trying to be strong and brave--the kind of woman her best friend respected and didn't pity.

"Starting now, Amber Thompson's eyes will be kept wide-open," she said. "No more ignoring facts. No more surprises. No more secrets."

A SEDAN PULLED up the driveway and Amber walked outside, heading off Mary Alice and her sister, Liz, the town's two biggest gossips. They were peering over the edge of the gulch at the tendrils of smoke. Gossip time.

Amber had managed to dodge Scott's meat loaf offer and had instead spent the past half hour prepping herself for the inevitable onslaught of gossipers. She planned to downplay what had happened here and on TV. She would control the message and image they spread about her and her failed relationship with Russell.

Easy.

"Hey, what's up?" she called, running her hands down the thighs of her jeans as she met up with them on the driveway.

"Amber, hon." Mary Alice pulled her into a massive hug, squeezing her against her massive bosom, a tin of mints digging into Amber's collarbone through their jackets. The woman didn't smell like herself without her usual cigarette scent, but she'd given it up after a medical scare earlier that year.

Amber broke free, rubbing the sore spot. "Mary Alice, you have to stop carrying mints in your bra. You're a danger to all that you hug and you hug aplenty."

Liz asked Amber, "Are you okay?"

"It's just a bruise," she replied, rubbing the spot.

"I meant…" Liz gestured to the cliff "…what happened?"

"Oh, just a mishap," she said dismissively. This was where she had to tread carefully. Anything she said to Liz could end up in the local paper, seeing as the woman wrote articles for them when she wasn't working in John Abcott's law office.

"We brought you some food," Mary Alice said, directing Amber to the sedan, which was hopefully loaded to the gills with chocolate. "We'll feed you and get you feeling as right as rain again."

"Actually, I'm okay," Amber replied.

"I read Russell's new book today," Liz said. "But I really don't understand you running his 'writing cave,' as he called it, over the side of the mountain. Seems a bit much."

It was a trap. Liz wanted her to defend herself and in the process tell her too much.

"It was an accident," Amber said carefully. "I was trying to move it for him."

"I don't blame her," Mary Alice said. "He put her in a book. All her private thoughts and dreams. Right there, exposed for the world."

Amber's legs lost their strength. "All of them?"

"And it's okay that you love Sir Studly. I mean Scott. We've all known it for some time." She patted Amber's hand as though she was distressed--which she was.

"I'm not--we're not--we're *friends*."

What had Russell said in his book? And why was Mary Alice referring to Scott as Sir Studly?

"Oh, it's really not a big shocker," Mary Alice said. "Don't worry, Amber. And his mother likes you just fine."

"But I--"

"Now," Liz said, eyebrows raised hopefully, "with Russell out of the picture and things out in the open about your feelings, are the two of you finally going to start dating?"

"Actually, Liz, I wanted you to be the first to hear that we eloped earlier today," Amber deadpanned, not quite believing the direction the conversation had gone. Scott was her best friend. Had they all lost their minds?

"You did?" Liz exclaimed, hands clasped over her chest.

"She's joking," Mary Alice said, smacking her sister's shoulder. "Come, dear." She placed an arm around Amber. "Let's feed you."

"I'm okay, really. Russell and I were never meant to be. Our breakup was mutual. We're both going off in different directions right now. He's an author and I'm... I'm, um..."

She really should have stuck with her script.

"That's what everyone says after they've run their ex's mobile office off the side of a cliff. You must feel as light as the mountain breeze right now," Mary Alice chirped, pushing what looked like one of Benny's chocolate maven pies into Amber's hands.

"Is this from Benny's?" Amber asked, lifting the plastic lid. It was. Her mother had worked at Benny's Big Burger since before Amber was born, having never used her beauty school training. Whenever Amber was down and out Benny's chef, Leif, gave her a slice of chocolate pie and a tall glass of milk on the house. It was one of the best things about growing up in a small town.

A "*Whoop!*" sounded behind them as they headed toward the house. Scott flashed his emergency lights in greeting.

"What's he up to? He's going to be late for meat loaf night," Mary Alice muttered. She raised her voice so Scott could hear. "It's chocolate therapy time, honey. I'm not sure with that testosterone of yours that you're equipped for this."

He grinned, but instead of joining them he called out his window, waving a stack of envelopes held by a rubber band. "Amber's mail. Thought she might want it."

Liz snatched it from his hands. "Very thoughtful. Now get going. Your mother is waiting."

"You sure you don't want to join us, Amber?" Scott asked, looking pointedly at the two sisters, who were determined to get her inside lickety-split so they could start pumping her for gossip.

Amber waved him away. She had everything under control and the sooner she redirected the gossipers from what could be seen as the explosive disintegration of her life, the better. With a shake of his head, Scott backed down the driveway. He made a phone signal with his thumb and pinky, letting her know he'd bail her out if the sisters got to be too much.

Amber had the best friend ever.

She ushered the women to the house. "Come in or you'll start feeding the mosquitoes."

"I heard they bite," Liz replied, as her sister added, "Not at all tame."

"Come in already and quit feeding the wildlife," Amber said from the doorway.

"Have you seen Jen lately?" Liz asked, referring to Amber's friend Jen Kulak who ran a guiding business out of Wally's Sporting Goods. Last summer she'd been involved in a forest fire investigation and had fallen in love with the investigator, Rob Raine.

Liz, making herself at home in the kitchen, gathered plates and forks for pie. Amber wanted to tell her to skip the plates, since they'd undoubtedly be finishing the whole thing and might as well eat straight from the dish.

"Rumor is she's pregnant," Liz said.

The sisters were going to bait and switch. Warm Amber up with other gossip, disarm her, then get her talking about herself before she noticed.

Nope. No way. Her lips were zipped. Nothing was coming out of her mouth unless it was part of her plan.

"Oh, they've been saying that for months," Mary Alice said. "Ever since she moved in with Rob. But I'll bet she's knocked up before Amber manages to move back to the city."

"I'll take that bet," her sister said.

"Hey, I'm not sure I appreciate the doubt in your tone in regards to my ability to leave this place," Amber interjected, taking the largest slice of pie for herself.

"I noticed your car was packed, and yet you are still here," Mary Alice pointed out.

"I still plan to go. Just maybe not immediately." Her rent was paid up at the moment and she'd have to see if she had enough for first and last month's rent on a place in the city before she hightailed it out of here, anyway.

"You know, Jen looked a bit green around the gills the other morning when I stopped by the store to get a football for my nephew," Mary Alice said thoughtfully.

Liz waggled a finger at her sister. "I'm going to win this one. You wait and see. Now, Nicola. She's lost a lot of weight." She spoke of their niece who had put on the Valentine's Day extravaganza and was a Blueberry Springs newcomer.

"She's working hard," Amber said between mouthfuls of pie. "The new subdivision's community development plans are keeping her busy."

"Do you think Jen will invite her family if she gets married?" Liz asked, backtracking the conversation to Jen's broken family. Her parents had split and used teenage Jen as leverage and, in the end, sent her to live with her boyfriend as she finished high school. The latest Amber had heard, the family was finally talking but she still didn't expect Mr. Kulak to walk Jen down an aisle any time soon.

Kind of like how Amber didn't expect her own father, Philip Powers, to walk her down the aisle. Wherever he was. She'd never met him, and by the sounds of it, never would. In any case, her mother had done a fine job of raising her on her own. Even if Amber were to meet him she wasn't sure what she'd say, but she knew it wouldn't be "Can you walk me down the aisle after leaving my mother high and dry, with no support whatsoever? What didn't you like about us anyway, you selfish jerk?"

So, she supposed she *did* know what she'd say to him, after all.

"Divorces can be so tricky when it comes to weddings," Mary Alice said.

"I don't blame her if she doesn't ask him," Amber replied. "I won't be inviting my dad to *my* wedding."

Amber licked chocolate off the back of her fork and wondered if it would be rude to help herself to a second slice of pie before the others had finished their first. "Philip will just miss out on the fatherly privilege of walking me down the aisle," she added.

"Philip?" Mary Alice asked, scraping the last of the mousse off her plate. She shared a confused glance with her sister.

"You know, the man who knocked up my mom, then ran off before I was even born?"

"Oh, would you look at the time," Liz said, standing up. "We need to get ready for the community watch meeting."

"Oh!" Mary Alice sat straighter. "How did I forget? I hope you're feeling better, Amber. I'm sorry we didn't get a chance to chat more. You should consider helping us with the bake sale-- we're raising funds for a new bus for the seniors' home."

"Wait," Amber said, holding up her hands as though trying to stop traffic. The women ignored her, quickly tidying up their plates and forks. "What happened to my dad?" The sisters said nothing, simply moved faster.

Mary Alice patted Amber's arm. "I just hadn't heard his name in so long. If you want to talk about Russell give me a call. I'll put on tea."

"There's nothing to say," Amber said, clicking into her rehearsed speech. "The book isn't about me. I was just helping him out when he wrote it. It's no big deal."

The sisters turned at the door, giving her a look that told her she was failing to move them off their predetermined gossip path. They knew the truth about her and Russell as inherently as if it had happened to them.

The sisters left and Amber wondered what that shared glance had been about. Her asking about Philip Powers had definitely scared them off. If there really had been a community watch meeting they would have tried to convince her to join, as usual.

They hadn't said a thing, but Amber could have sworn they didn't think Philip was her father. But how could that be? Knowing who your dad was wasn't something a person normally got wrong.

She flicked through her mind's rolodex of memories. Her mother had never once corrected her the few times Amber had referred to Philip as her father, while dancing around the taboo subject of her parentage. Then again, she couldn't recall her mom ever out-and-out stating that he was.

What did it mean?

If he wasn't her father, was everyone she knew keeping secrets from her? Did everyone believe she was the most naïve and gullible person in the world?

Because when it came right down to it, if the town's biggest gossips believed Philip wasn't her dad… he wasn't.

A VEHICLE PULLED up Amber's driveway and, assuming it was another gawker coming to check out the scene of the trailer's death, she kept working at the kitchen table, head down, trying not to think about the layers of deception she'd been living under for months and possibly even years.

"How long are you planning to hide out?" her mother asked, entering the kitchen and setting a casserole dish on the table.

Amber jumped. "Technically, I'm not hiding out," she said, "just catching up on database work."

Her mom waited, hands on her hips.

Amber had to look away, afraid to think that her mother had allowed her to believe a lie all her life. She trusted her, but if her mother had deceived her, then what other lies about her life did Amber still unknowingly believe?

"I'm not going to town again until everyone has forgotten about me," she said.

"The gossip isn't that bad."

"Yeah, right. Mary Alice and Liz were here last night and already had their minds made up about how everything went down." Amber sighed and rubbed her forehead, still mad at herself for how trusting and blind she'd been.

Her mom smiled. "Sounds like them."

"Everyone's read the book, haven't they?" It had been out a mere twenty-four hours and Amber had had a ton of texts and phone calls about it from people in town. So far, she had ignored every single one of them. "He got me all wrong."

"You read it?"

"Of course. I have to know what I'm defending," Amber said.

"It wasn't that bad. He got your charm right, I think."

"*You* read it?" Ugh. There were scenes in there she definitely didn't want her mother reading.

"Yes, and I brought you chocolate drops." She pulled a cellophane package out of her shoulder bag and set it on the table. Which meant the book *was* that bad. Although the chocolate could also be a sympathy gift due to her recent breakup, or for the accidental recreational vehicle manslaughter.

"My hips thank you."

"What's wrong?"

"Nothing."

"You seem upset."

"It's nothing." Amber debated asking her mother about Philip. She wanted to believe what she'd always believed, but had promised herself that there would be no more secrets in her life. But if she found out her mother had lied about Philip, how many other secrets would come pouring out? Amber wasn't sure she was ready to deal with a complete life upheaval.

Her mom sat across from her, hands folded, waiting for her to unload.

Amber closed her laptop and pushed it to the side, then wished she'd kept it as a barrier between them. Gloria had always avoided and dodged the subject of Philip with determination similar to that of a running back on his way to the end zone.

"The trailer really was an accident," Amber said.

"And so you're mad?"

"I'm upset because Russell kept so many secrets from me…" She watched her mother for her reaction. Maybe she was simply waiting for Amber to bring up the subject so she could lay everything out in the open. Or maybe the gossips were wrong for once.

Gloria eased back in the chair, but said nothing.

"And I feel as though I don't really know myself any longer," Amber added.

Her mother tipped her head to the side, watching her.

It was now or never.

"Mary Alice and Liz each gave me a funny look when I mentioned Philip yesterday."

"Oh?" Her mom got up and began straightening items on the kitchen counter, a sure sign that she was nervous.

"It was almost as though they didn't believe he was my father." Amber watched her mother's back. Her busy moves ceased for a split second.

"Is there insurance on Russell's holiday trailer? I can't imagine one of those things being cheap even though it was an older, secondhand one."

Her mother was keeping something from her. Something about Amber's dad. Something vital.

Amber felt as though her world was deep, shifting sand and she no longer had solid ground to stand upon.

AMBER RINSED out her teacup and, through the kitchen window, watched Scott pull up the driveway in his police truck. He got out slowly, assessing the yard as though on the lookout for clues, his badge winking in the early April sunshine. He ambled slowly to her door, his gait relaxed in a way that said he was in charge and nothing could faze him. No wonder he was the one steady presence in her life.

The only person who didn't keep secrets from her. The one man who might be able to help her get to the bottom of her life, then help her up again.

He knocked twice, then let himself in.

"I'm in the kitchen, Officer Malone," she called, meeting him in the entry with a big smile.

"I love it when you call me that," he said, with a mischievous twinkle in his eyes. They grew more serious as they roved over her. "How are you today?"

"Fine." She was still upset about Russell putting her in a book, but not nearly as bothered about him breaking up with her as she thought she should be. Maybe the unexpected grand event of both the book and trailer was overshadowing the emotional fallout of the breakup. Or, even more odd, maybe she was okay with him being out of her life. She'd always felt as though she had to work to be bright, funny, and everything he needed. Add in the fact that the man was a usurious schmuck and it was a case of well-timed good riddance.

Seeming satisfied with his assessment and her answer, Scott moved past her, his fingers drifting over her hip so he probably wouldn't knock her over. Shivers ran through her at his touch and she shut the outer door, following him into the house. "I hear the ladies brought you pie the other day," he said from the kitchen. "Any left?"

"Nope."

His lips twisted into a pouty frown, which undoubtedly got him what he wanted from women 99 percent of the time.

"Did you really think there'd be any?"

"A guy can hope."

"Scott?"

"Yeah?"

Amber paused, thinking. He knew things. He was one of those quiet, protective sorts that people confessed to--even when he was out of uniform. If anyone knew who her father was, it would be him.

"If I ask you something, do you promise to tell me the truth?"

Scott was quiet for a long moment, then his gaze drifted up, meeting hers. "Always."

"Do you know who my father is?"

Scott blinked slowly. "Come again?"

"That's what she said."

He snorted at her lame, off-color joke.

"Come on, that was a perfect setup for an innuendo," Amber said, hoisting herself onto the kitchen counter so she'd be closer to eye level with her best friend. "So? Do you? I'm getting the vibe that it's not Philip Powers."

"Right."

Amber felt as though every molecule in the room had stopped moving. "What do you mean, 'right'?"

She watched him for a moment as he struggled with what to say.

"You *knew* it wasn't Philip and you never told me?" Amber exclaimed. She gave him an outraged glare, reaching out to give his chest a massive shove, sending herself off the counter and into Scott's arms instead. "Some friend you are."

He braced his hands under her elbows. "I don't know who your father is. For all I know it really is Philip and the gossips have it wrong."

"They never have it wrong! Not on something huge like this."

"Why are you asking about this? Why now?"

"Why not now? I can't believe you didn't tell me. I thought you were the one person..." She thumped his chest when he refused to let her go. "The one person, Scott."

"Amber." His grip was firm as he held her in front of him, his voice rough. "What I hear at work is confidential. If I thought this was worth pursuing I would have told you."

"How can it not be worth pursuing? We're talking about my *father*."

"Sometimes secrets need to be kept."

"What do you know that you're not telling me?"

Scott gave a frustrated sigh, finally releasing her to push a hand through his hair.

"What?"

"Nothing. Just take a moment and think outside yourself. Why would anyone keep your father a secret from you for several decades?"

"Because, apparently, that's what people do. They keep secrets from me because they think I can't handle it. Well, guess what, world, I can handle it."

Scott leaned against the counter, his expression thoughtful, as if he was sizing her up. "Secrets are secrets," he said, "because people don't want them known. It's not our business to unearth them. They're secrets for a reason."

"They're secrets about *me*, Scott. They affect *me*." She was hanging off his collar, begging. "They're about my life and I deserve to know. You know who your father is, but imagine not knowing. It's like part of you is a mystery. Unanswered. Unexplainable."

Scott carefully pried her fingers from his shirt. The sound of another vehicle coming up the driveway distracted Amber.

"Is that Dr. Leham?" she asked, pointing to the shiny BMW that had pulled up in front of the house. Why would he be visiting her? Maybe his new girlfriend--Amber's long-time friend Katie Reiter--had borrowed it and was coming by to see how she was doing.

"He's got a newer model," Scott said, leaning against Amber's back to get a better look out the window. His body was a warm and comforting presence and she resisted pressing against him. Scott had been the one constant in her life, but she needed to remember that even he had been keeping secrets from her.

She turned to face him, realizing that if her mother had been lying, something must have gone incredibly wrong.

"Scott? Do you have secrets? I mean more secrets? More than just the Philip thing."

"Everyone has secrets, Amber."

Not the answer she wanted.

"Did you ever tell your mom about what really happened when you bent the bumper of her car?" he asked.

"I meant that you're keeping about me, my life."

Scott's eyes narrowed as he glared out the window, his hands going protectively to her shoulders.

"What?"

She turned, spotting Russell and his editor, Sabrina, walking up to the house. Outrage cut through Amber and she didn't know whether to run and hide or come out fighting.

"What does he want?" Scott grumbled, moving swiftly to the front door to head him off.

Amber hesitated, then followed. Scott opened the door before Russell could knock or let himself in. Seeing Sabrina in her lithe linen outfit standing behind Russell made Amber glad to have Scott as her own personal backup.

"I'm here for my stuff," Russell said.

"There is no reason for you to be here unannounced," Scott said, arms crossed, acting as a human wall between Amber and her ex.

"I need my trailer. My stuff."

"And you plan to pull it with that?" Scott asked, tipping his chin toward the sports car.

"The trailer might be a problem," Amber murmured.

"I have a friend coming with a truck in a few minutes. He'll tow it."

Scott faced Amber. "Are you going to tell him, or should I?"

"It didn't take you long to move on." Russell smirked.

"You called that one," Sabrina whispered to him, eyeing Scott with what looked like hunger.

"Move on?" Amber stepped in front of Scott, rage boiling through her. "*Move on?* You moved on to her while I was still in your bed."

Sabrina looked away, a flush tingeing her cheeks.

"Still stuck in the friend zone, huh?" Russell said to Scott. "Sorry, pal."

Amber lunged at him, but Scott held her back. "Not worth it," he stated. "I'm sure karma will have a heyday and do a more effective job than we ever could."

When Russell stepped closer to the door, Scott widened his stance, arms crossed, blocking him. "You're not coming in. Not now. Not ever."

"I paid half the rent this month. Therefore, yes I am."

"Do I need to issue a restraining order on Amber's behalf? She doesn't want you here. She's removed everything of yours. You left, *pal.*"

"I need to make sure she got everything." Russell laid a hand on Scott's chest, trying to push him out of the way. But he had the writer's arm twisted and pinned behind him in a matter of seconds, his face smushed into the doorjamb.

"Were you trying to assault a police officer?" Scott growled in his ear. "That's a court appearance and wouldn't be good publicity at this point in time. You might be a newscaster on sabbatical, but remember, Amber comes from a small town. She's good friends with local reporters and a story like this wouldn't stay local for very long."

Amber bit her bottom lip so she wouldn't smile. She loved Scott so very much at this moment.

"You know where your trailer is?" Amber was half excited, half nervous. She pointed to the edge of the cliff, her finger shaking. "It kind of became a lesson in physics for me. Sorry. I hope you didn't have anything important in it. Other than everything of yours that I put in there first."

Russell and Sabrina followed her finger, their faces pinched in confusion. Finally, comprehension dawned.

"You pushed my trailer off the edge of a cliff?" Russell's voice was high and scratchy.

Amber crossed her arms. "It was an accident. However, I don't think your lies, cheating, or basing a fictional character on me was."

Scott released Russell and the man massaged his shoulder, moving down the front steps, putting a safe buffer between them.

"This isn't over, Amber," Russell said, his voice shaking with anger.

"I say it is," Scott retorted.

Amber spoke over Scott's shoulder. "You're right. I think I still owe you one for all of the secrets you kept from me."

As Russell and Sabrina backed up the Beemer moments later, Amber turned to Scott. "No more secrets. I'm going to find out who my father is. And if you're the friend you say you are, help me."

2

Amber decided enough was enough. She'd hinted around for days about Philip and yet her mother had revealed nothing but obvious discomfort.

There had to be something there. There had to be more. And if Amber was going to get to the bottom of the secrets and figure out who she was, then she needed to somehow force Gloria to tell her the truth. Amber was a grown-up. She could handle it. Both of them could.

And then there was Scott. He had promised to help, but hadn't come up with a thing she hadn't so far. Which was nothing.

She'd half hoped he had a secret parental database he could hack into, revealing, with a lovely flourish, the name of her father. But apparently the police didn't have one of those, and even if they did it wouldn't be ethical or legal to use it for personal reasons. Blah, blah, blah. Scott and his sound morals. She loved him for it, but it was driving her crazy.

Her mother had finished her shift at the restaurant half an hour ago and Amber knocked on her door, knowing she would be home.

Sure enough, she answered, at first looking pleased to see Amber, then appearing cautious. "Everything okay?" she asked.

Amber debated the merits of going soft on her versus cutting to the chase. She decided for honest, but not super-blunt. "I thought we could chat."

"Was Russell upset about the trailer? I heard he knows now."

"Can I come in?"

As if realizing she was blocking the door, Gloria opened it wider, allowing her to come in. "I was just going to have a cup of tea. Would you like one?"

Amber waited for her to finish brewing the tea, then sat with her at the small kitchen table.

"Philip isn't my father, is he?"

Her mother was silent for a long time and Amber thought she was going to refuse to answer. But finally she shook her head.

The truth struck Amber as hard as if she hadn't been expecting it. She struggled to stay neutral, unemotional, but her voice cracked when she asked, "Who is he?"

Gloria studied the tabletop, lips pulled tight between her teeth. After a moment she opened her mouth as though about to say something, then closed it again. "I can't tell you."

"Why not?"

"It's… complicated," her mother said.

"I've become quite good with complicated."

"It will change things, Amber, and I don't think it's a good idea." She stood up, clearing away their cups even though they'd barely touched them. "Things are good enough the way they are."

"Please, Mom."

Amber needed to know.

Gloria let out a sigh, suddenly looking aged beyond her years, and for a second Amber saw the woman's life in a flash. A single mom, a waitress, raising her daughter the best she could in a gossipy small town. It took a village to raise a child, and Blueberry Springs had definitely helped. Benny, her mother's boss, acting like a father figure. His chef, Leif, taking her in and feeding her after school while listening to her chat about her day when her mother was busy waiting tables. Her friend Mandy Mattson's mom taking her to extracurricular events on Thursday nights while Gloria pulled her weekly double shift.

It couldn't have been easy. And now to have her daughter on the wrong side of an award-winning newscaster who was used to digging out hidden truths behind locked borders. Russell even still had a limp from being shot while working on an overseas cover-up. He was a public hero who would beat Amber to the punch when it came to defending herself and her character. What chance did she and her mother have of becoming more than what they were in this moment?

"Please. Just a name. I've always thought it was Philip, and it's driving me crazy to think I believed something that was wrong my whole entire life. I feel like I don't know who I am."

"Amber…" Her mother's tone of voice was a warning, but Amber ignored it.

"I can handle it. I can handle the truth."

"I don't…" Gloria sighed. "I'll think about it."

Her mother never said no, just "I'll think about it," which meant "go away and forget about it because I'm not saying yes."

"Please? I can keep a secret. I won't tell a soul, I promise."

Her mom braced her hands on the counter and dropped her head. "This isn't about you."

"It was so long ago. Nobody will care." Amber felt desperate. The more her mother blocked her, the more certain she became that knowing who her father was would help her understand why she had tricked herself into believing a man like Russell was The One. And if she knew who she was, she could prevent herself from falling into traps like that again.

"He's going to care," Gloria said, her voice hoarse with held-back emotion. "Believe me."

Amber felt the slam of rejection all over again. Her father

didn't want her. He didn't want anyone to know his mistake, and it didn't matter if the man was Philip or someone else. Rejection was rejection.

AMBER FELT DEFEATED AND UNTETHERED. She no longer had the image of the mysterious Philip, her deadbeat dad, residing in the back of her mind. Now there was a big, open question mark. A man who would be bothered if Amber knew who he was.

Was he someone she knew? Was that why her mother was so intent on protecting him? In Amber's books, he certainly didn't deserve it, and she needed to know who she was supposed to direct her angst and feelings of rejection toward.

Unable to concentrate on fixing a non-urgent bug in a work database, Amber closed her laptop. She would earn her paycheck by telecommuting later. Right now she needed to talk to her mother.

Daring to brave any gossip about her and Russell that might still be swirling through the atmosphere, she decided to head to town once again in a quest for information.

Her car started, then sputtered and died. She got the old beater running again, producing a cloud of smoke so black and thick that she feared someone would call the fire department. Amber tentatively put the car in reverse, coaxing it back a few feet before the engine died again. She was going to need a different set of wheels.

The backhoe was still parked near the cliff's edge, as she'd been too afraid to move it, and she considered driving it to town, before discarding the idea.

Amber tapped her thigh, thinking, as she took in the craggy mountain view. How was she going to afford fixing her car and saving up to move back to the city, when she had to pay the full rent on the house now that Russell was gone? She hadn't wanted to return to Blueberry Springs, but he'd insisted it was the place to write his book.

She turned her gaze to the machine shed. She'd had to climb over a motorized cart of some kind to reach the backhoe. Surely Rosalind wouldn't mind her borrowing a vehicle to get around. Amber opened the building's massive doors, allowing light to streak across the dirt floor, which smelled of spilled oil, earth, and stale air.

It was a golf cart. She kicked the tires while circling it. The key was in the ignition and she slid onto the cracked seat. Finding the choke, she pulled it out, then gingerly pumped the gas pedal twice and, holding her breath, turned the key.

A weak whine came from the engine.

She turned the key again and the motor let out a few halfhearted, unconvincing chugs, but refused to turn over. Keeping the key cranked to the right, Amber finessed the gas pedal with her toe, flooring it to drain the extra gas from the carburetor when it seemed flooded, then pumping it once more, hoping the battery would hold out through the effort. She pushed in the choke, then pulled it out halfway when the machine chugged and protested.

"Come on, baby. Come on."

Finally the engine coughed and sputtered, almost leveling out before falling into a death-throe unevenness that had Amber yanking on the choke and pumping the gas pedal again.

"Don't do this. Don't make me walk."

A few more sputters and the cart's rumbling and coughing eased into a quiet hum and tick, punctuated by the odd hiccup and gasoline-laden fart.

Oh, thank goodness. There were bears out there. She wanted wheels.

A few minutes later she was gliding down the mountain toward town, wondering why she hadn't thought of driving a golf cart as her get-around vehicle before. There was plenty of room for groceries and even a passenger, plenty of fresh air, and the fuel economy had to be excellent.

As she turned into town she caught Scott giving her a second glance from behind a hedge, where he stood with his radar gun.

A speed trap. Well. That was surely going to ruffle some feathers. She waved as she drove past, her heart skipping a beat as he popped up to watch her pass. But Amber was determined not to give him time to figure out whether her mode of transportation was street legal.

She parked in the alley behind Benny's restaurant and entered through the back door, crossing the small staff room before peeking out to see if she could spot her mom serving the midafternoon coffee crowd.

"Amber, you look hungry." The chef, Leif, ushered her into the kitchen. He cut her a slice of the semi-famous chocolate pie he made daily and had put Benny's on the map for most women in the area. He poured Amber a glass of milk and his cologne reminded her of the hours she'd spent watching him cook while she waited for Gloria to finish her shift. Without a word Amber shoveled a large bite of chocolate into her mouth and savored its decadent richness. Nothing better in the world.

"Still your favorite?" Leif asked.

She broke off another piece with her fork and said, "Are you fishing for compliments? You know your pie's up there with Mandy's brownies."

"Who do you think taught her to bake? She wasn't just a waitress during her years here."

Mandy Mattson had won the town's Fall Fair for years with her old brownie recipe, but when she'd quit waitressing and opened her own Wrap It Up restaurant, she'd upped her game and changed her brownie recipe to a whiskey-and-gumdrop one that had solidified her status as an automatic blue ribbon shoe-in. The new brownies were responsible for at least ten of the pounds riding on Amber's hips.

"My pie hasn't won any awards," Leif said thoughtfully.

"Have you entered it in a contest?"

He smiled and wiped his hands on a tea towel. Of course he hadn't.

"Did you ever get your online recipe forum working properly?" Amber asked. "I'm making the chocolate chip squares in the squares section for the seniors' bake sale."

"Those are good. And no, I'm still getting some odd glitches."

"The same ones?"

He nodded.

"I think I came across a solution the other day while doing some research for something else. Want me to try and fix it?"

"Free pie for life if you do."

Amber laughed. "Sounds good." She was already getting free pie just by being Gloria's daughter. "Hey, can I ask you something?"

"Anything."

"How long have you and Mom worked together?" Amber stuck her plate and fork in the commercial dishwasher, along with her empty milk glass.

The chef stared at the ceiling for a moment before replying, "Fifteen. No, fourteen years. You loved my pie even then."

"Women love anything with chocolate, so don't let it go to your head," she joked, stirring a pot simmering on the stove. It looked like spaghetti was tonight's special. Maybe if the place wasn't too busy she'd stick around. She'd finished her mother's casserole and didn't feel like getting back into the habit of cooking for one.

"Get away from that. You aren't wearing a hairnet." Leif shooed her back, then snatched her hand, inspecting the fingernails she'd chewed down to the quick. "You need to relax. Look at your hands."

Amber tucked her fingers and their lack of lovely nails into the pocket of her hoodie. "Did you know my mom before you started working here?"

"Nope."

Nuts. "Did she ever say anything about the man she--"

Gloria entered the kitchen and froze. "What's going on?"

"Hi, Mom. Just hanging out with Leif."

Her mother addressed the chef. "We need a grilled cheese and a tuna salad." She moved around the kitchen, slicing pie and scooping fruit salad into a small bowl as though everything was normal, but Amber could tell her mother knew what she was up to and wasn't too happy about it.

"What's up?" Leif asked, giving both of them a look. As an ex-police officer, he was good at catching undercurrents between the two of them.

"Amber, why don't we go to the staff room," her mother said. "We can chat for a moment before these orders are up. I'll be back in a jiff, Leif. Call me if you need me."

In the small room, Gloria hissed to Amber, "Not here and not now."

"You don't even know why I'm here."

"I told you I can't tell you."

"I promise I won't tell anyone. Please? I'm desperate."

"I said no. Your father doesn't know, so just drop it." Her mother's mouth formed a fine line as she hurried out of the staff room.

Amber blinked away the shock of that statement. "He doesn't know?" she called, hurrying to the doorway. By the time she reached it, her mother was already gone.

How could he not know? How did you keep a secret like that in Blueberry Springs?

You didn't. Which meant he didn't live in Blueberry Springs. That would also explain why nobody knew who he was. They weren't covering for her mother--they simply didn't know.

Hang on. If her father didn't know Amber existed, then he couldn't have rejected her.

She smiled. She hadn't been rejected by him.

She let the feeling sink in. It felt good. Really good.

He could be somewhere right now, wishing he had a daughter… and here she was.

She had to find him. Had to.

She hustled through the back of the restaurant with renewed purpose. If he wasn't in Blueberry Springs, no harm, no foul. She could find out who he was without him even knowing. Nothing more perfect than that.

Benny walked by and, seeing Amber, said, "Your mom's working a double today. I think I just saw her take an order out."

"Thanks."

"You okay?" he asked, stopping Amber from entering the dining room.

"Yeah. Fine."

"You sure? You look… happy."

Amber did a double take. "Shouldn't I be happy?"

Through the dining room's swinging doors she spotted her mother handing a young couple crayons and coloring mats for their kids, settling people in, doing her job. She didn't look happy. Far from it. She looked scared and worried.

Amber couldn't ask her for more. She couldn't push Gloria through this, but had to find another way. Which meant she had to keep a secret from her mom.

A secret for a secret.

"You didn't have to turn that smile upside down," Benny complained.

"Benny? My mom didn't ever tell you who my father is, did she?"

The restaurant owner stroked his double chin, watching her. "Can't say that she did."

Amber sighed.

"In time, kid." He squeezed her shoulder. "Say, did you hear Scott's leaving town?"

"What?" Blood rushed in Amber's ears.

"He's applying out. A promotion of sorts. I'm surprised he didn't tell you."

Amber's mind stuck in neutral. Secrets.

More secrets.

She'd even asked him if he had secrets and he hadn't told her he was leaving.

What was she going to do in town without him? He couldn't leave her here. She was supposed to be the one going.

"Sorry about Russell," Benny said quietly, looking uncomfortable.

"The book isn't true," Amber replied automatically. "It's not about me."

The older man smiled, relaxing. "Oh, good. Well, have a nice day, Amber. Enjoy that sunshine."

Right. She'd do that while she went and gave Scott a piece of her mind for keeping his secret from her. The man was supposed to be on her side. He was supposed to be different.

"Scott?" Amber tapped his shoulder and he popped out of the bush, fumbling his radar gun.

"Amber, never sneak up on an on-duty officer. I'm armed and trained to kill."

"Right. So? When were you going to tell me you're leaving?"

His spine straightened as he turned the speed gun in the direction of an oncoming car, looking uncharacteristically guilty. Amber placed her hand in front of its sensor.

"Amber, quit interfering with police procedure."

"Why didn't you tell me? Why did you keep it a secret?" Her

voice held a tremor, betraying how upset she was. "I even asked if you had any secrets and you *lied*."

"I didn't lie. I told you everyone has secrets. The fact that I had applied out was mine."

"I trusted you. I thought we were friends. Friends who didn't keep secrets from each other." Amber turned, storming away.

A few quick steps and Scott had caught up, snagging her arm, stopping her. "I haven't even had an interview yet. You didn't tell me you were dating that jerk Russell until you were moving in with him. Here. In Blueberry Springs."

Amber ripped herself from his grasp. "That was different."

"How?" he demanded, his eyes glinting with something she didn't quite understand.

"I knew you wouldn't approve," she whispered, trying to blink away the stinging in her eyes. She'd known Scott wouldn't like Russell and still she'd dated Russell, moved in with him and allowed him the opportunity to betray her. And then she'd expected Scott to pick up the pieces like always.

"I'm not perfect, okay? And I'm never going to find a man you approve of."

"How could a woman like you ever convince yourself that it was a smart thing to hook up with a man like Russell?"

"What's that supposed to mean?" Scott woke up next to incredible women who fell at his feet. He had no idea what Amber's options were like.

"You knew I wouldn't approve. You said you knew it wasn't love and yet you wasted your time with a man like him. You could have missed being with someone worthy of your love. Someone who would treat you right." Scott's voice grew more gentle. "Someone who loves you back. Someone you can trust."

There was heat and love in his eyes when Amber finally looked up. Her heart raced as she laid a trembling hand against his cheek, noting that he didn't lean into her touch despite his words. The almost-kiss they'd almost shared on Valentine's Day had changed him. Changed both of them. If Russell hadn't shown up in time, would she have ruined her lifelong friendship with Scott by kissing him? Or would things have been okay? Or, dare she imagine it, even more than okay?

She was kidding herself. She wasn't in love with her best friend and his crush was just that--a crush. Scott dated mayors, not women who had been humiliated on national television. Her best friend, despite all their history and their closeness, was out of her league, and she was delusional if she thought he was hinting that he should be her boyfriend because he could love her better than anyone else.

And if he really did want her, he wouldn't be leaving. Her. The town. Their friendship.

"Why are you doing this?" Amber whispered, still holding his cheek, seeking understanding.

"Amber," he said, breaking away, heading back to his post, his expression closed and dark, "it's just a job application."

"For a job that would take you away from Blueberry Springs." *Away from me.*

"As a good friend of mine is always telling me," he said over his shoulder, "there is more to life than Blueberry Springs."

"Yeah?" Her voice shook. "Well, that life sucks." She stomped to her golf cart, glancing over her shoulder to see if Scott was following her. He wasn't. Because if he'd loved her he would have swept her into a dip and kissed her senseless. And he didn't love her, so he hadn't.

Instead, he called from his spot by the bush, "If it's not so great, then why are you trying to go back to it?"

Unable to think of a good reply, she simply sped away in her cart, wishing the thing could at least peel rubber to give her a better exit.

Amber woke up with her face stuck to the keyboard. Scott was leaving. He was leaving Blueberry Springs. Leaving her.

She tried to rub out the key imprints pressed into her cheek as she checked the time. She felt hollow. If Scott wasn't here, then what was the point?

Pushing aside her feelings of dejection, she figured she needed to get moving. It was early enough that she could still grab a breakfast sandwich at Mandy's and possibly avoid most of the town's gossips, plus get her baking to the seniors' fund-raising bake sale on time.

As she got ready to drive into town thoughts of her father kept whirling through her mind. If she knew who he was, maybe she would understand herself better. Maybe she'd figure out why she didn't date nice guys like Scott, but went for men like Russell, who were an express pass to unhappiness and betrayal.

But to find her dad, she'd have to keep secrets, and she didn't want more of them in her life. She hadn't known about Russell's secrets, and they'd turned her upside down. What other secrets were out there ready to trip her up?

Taking the golf cart, Amber rolled down the mountain and into town. Blueberry Springs was idyllic at this time of day and she waved to Beth Reiter, who was bouncing her toddler son in her arms while pacing her front porch.

Amber continued on to Main Street, slowing to watch Scott help Elsie from the nursing home up onto the curb in front of the hair salon, his badge shining in the early sunshine.

The town would miss him. Amber would miss him. He glanced up at her, giving her a nod as she passed. She quickly looked away, hoping he'd think she hadn't seen him, and that he wouldn't notice the unexplained tears brimming in her eyes.

Toward the end of Main there was hubbub in front of Benny's restaurant. Distracted by what was going on, she nearly ran over a man who'd hurried into the street, stopping right in front of her. He had a large camera slung over his shoulder and aimed its lens so it was facing her dead-on. She froze, unsure what to do about the unexpected blockade. A reporter joined the cameraman, coming a few steps closer, microphone extended as though ready to ward off a hungry lion.

"Amber Thompson, what do you have to say about being the main character in Russell Peaks's runaway bestseller, *Ember Unfolded?*"

"I am not the main character." Amber steered around the reporter, jerking to a stop as the town's police truck came to a halt in the oncoming lane, blocking her exit. Scott jumped out, hurrying to her side. She was half relieved to see him and half ticked off.

"Move along please, you're blocking traffic." Scott began shooing the reporter and cameraman off the road, while muttering to Amber, "I told you to stay home today."

"No, you didn't."

"I sent you a text."

Amber patted her pockets. Her phone wasn't with her. "Yeah, well, you're leaving, so you don't get to tell me what to do anymore."

"Like you ever listened in the first place," he grumbled.

"It's Sir Studly!" the reporter whispered loudly to the cameraman, pointing at Scott. The woman unconsciously smoothed her hair and straightened her spine, her eyes sparkling with delight.

Scott had become a stud, yes. However, she had really, really been hoping people wouldn't pick up on the fact that Russell had called him Sir Studly, the heroine's love interest in *Ember Unfolded.*

This was going to make a perfectly crappy day that much better, wasn't it?

The reporter gave her a gleeful, excited look and Amber sighed. Scott was wonderful, but the two of them weren't in love.

They were friends, as some things were much too important to ruin with complications such as hot, steamy sex.

Out of the corner of her eye she saw Mary Alice do a U-turn in the middle of the street to claim a parking spot on the opposite side. She climbed out and started heading their way, the sun streaking through the trees along the street giving her a dappled look.

"Mary Alice," Scott called to her. "I saw you pull that illegal move, and now you're jaywalking."

The woman rolled her eyes and kept walking, knowing those minor violations weren't enforced in Blueberry Springs and that Scott was just busting her chops so she wouldn't come see what the commotion was about.

"He's in a mood, Mary Alice," Amber called. "I think he has a quota to meet for his new job. You know, the one he's leaving us all for?"

"Would you quit it already?" Scott muttered.

"Officer Malone, how do you feel about being portrayed as the love interest in Russell Peaks's new book?" The reporter had come closer and had her microphone in Scott's face.

"It isn't him," Amber said, trying to usher the reporter and cameraman away from her friend. "There's really nothing to see here."

"Love interest?" Scott perked up, glancing at Amber for clues.

He was feeling playful now. Great. So he *was* feeling guilty for leaving, and was going to put on his Mr. Fun act so she'd end up laughing and thus forgive him.

Not on his life. Not this time.

"You didn't read the book?" Mary Alice was laughing. "Oh, honey! How did you miss this? You need to read it right quick. You're in it, just like Amber."

Amber shook her head and waved her hands, trying to convince the woman to cool it. "It's not him. It's not me. It's a work of fiction."

Grinning, Scott slung an arm around Amber's shoulders and gave her forehead a quick, chaste kiss. It made her flesh tingle, made her body want to turn in and ask for more, while trying to make sure his next kiss landed on her lips.

"Love interest, huh? What did you tell that jerk of a novelist about me, anyway?"

Amber made a feeble sound, noting that the reporter was excitedly talking into her microphone about a real life love story full of rivals and happily ever afters.

Amber pushed Scott away from her, ignoring the rush of sparks that sped up her arms where they touched. "He's just goofing around. Russell's book portrays nobody real. The disclaimer at the beginning even said so. It's a work of fiction. End of story."

"Aw. You don't find me sexy?" Scott did a little hip shimmy that made Amber blush.

"Enough," she muttered, smacking him in the chest. Him being sexy had nothing to do with this and he was going to blow things up rather than help them die down. "This isn't like the Blueberry Springs Greatest Couple competition. They'll get the wrong impression."

"They won as couple of the year, but were disqualified for not being a real couple," Mary Alice interjected for the benefit of the reporter. "On Valentine's Day."

"We were goofing around!" Amber insisted. "He was just trying to make me feel better."

"About Russell not being there," Mary Alice added. "He wasn't a very good boyfriend."

The reporter had placed her microphone in Amber's face again. "Is the rumor true that you destroyed author Russell Peaks's mobile writing office after you discovered he had left you for his editor?"

"I think we're done here," Scott said, suddenly dropping his playful demeanor and pushing the camera so it was aimed at the ground.

He led Amber away with a hand at the base of her spine as Mary Alice chanted, "Nothing to see here, move along. Nothing to see here. At least not any longer."

Liz had joined the small crowd that had gathered, and was trying to help, muttering things about Amber to the reporter that Amber wasn't so sure would be helpful.

"It is said you are looking for your long-lost father, Amber," called the reporter a few moments later.

Amber jerked to a stop, heart thundering in her chest. Her mother would never forgive her if her secrets got tied up in the Russell problem.

"Is there anything you'd like to say to him?" the reporter added softly, her hand over the microphone as Amber glanced back. "You could ask for information on air. Maybe we could help."

Liz gave her a hopeful look and Amber tried to stay calm. The woman meant well. It really wouldn't be worth going to jail over murdering her.

As Amber tried to think of a reply that would convince the reporter to drop the story, Scott whispered in her ear, his warm breath sending shivers down her spine, "Don't do it. I'll help you search from now until the end of time, just please don't do this."

Amber turned to the reporter, Scott's grip on her elbow tightening. "This is a private matter that has already been resolved. Thank you."

It was a partial lie, but she figured it was okay, seeing as, technically, on one level it *had* been resolved. Her mother wasn't going to tell her and Amber was still looking--without media assistance. Issue resolved.

As Amber climbed into her golf cart, Mary Alice whispered, "I guess you don't want to hear the old rumor about why your mother went away to hairdressing school?"

Amber processed the comment as she started the cart. It was a well-known fact that her mom had gone, but had never become a stylist—an odd little bump in her history that Amber had thought nothing of. Her mother had simply changed her mind after finding she didn't have an aptitude for styling hair. But the way Mary Alice was throwing out the hint, Amber knew there was more to the story.

Another family secret.

mber waited outside Benny's for her mother to be done her shift. She nursed a cup of take-out decaf coffee, going over her plan once again. Could she really woo her mom into revealing the hairdressing secret--assuming there was one? Amber wasn't certain, but she thought it was likely unrelated to her father, seeing as there were several years separating her mother going to hairdressing school and Amber being conceived.

Then again, with her mother? Who knew what the truth was. And if there even was a secret, it could be anything. An elopement. A baby. She could have accidentally burned someone's hair off and been sued. It could be anything. Or nothing at all.

And it was driving Amber crazy.

She sighed and continued to pace. It was late, after ten, by the time her mother came out, looking fatigued but happy.

"Amber! What are you doing here?"

"Just thought I'd walk you home."

Her mom gave her a suspicious look. "Why?"

"I was in town."

"And?"

"There were reporters here today and I wanted to make sure they weren't harassing you." A partial truth. That was the thing with secrets—they had an insidious nature and begot lies and more secrets. They were evil little things that should be staked through the heart.

"Did they bother you?" her mother asked quickly, moving closer.

"Scott chased them off."

"He's a good man."

Amber smiled, feeling warm down to her toes at the mention of her best friend. "He's going to make some lucky woman incredibly happy."

But he was leaving. Sadness washed over Amber and she caught her mother giving her a sidelong glance.

"What?"

"He's leaving." Amber let out a gusty sigh, having come to terms with the fact that it was pretty darn hypocritical of her to berate him for leaving when she had already done the same to him, and was planning on doing so again once she could get her life back in order.

"I heard. Sorry. But you're leaving again soon, too, aren't you?"

"Yeah, but." It felt different somehow. Scott wasn't supposed to leave. He was supposed to be a Blueberry Springs lifer.

Her mother gave her a half hug. "Shall we?" She gestured down the street, where pools of light from the streetlamps reminded Amber of hopscotch patterns she'd drawn on the sidewalk as a child.

"Did the reporters hassle you?" she asked again, wanting to ensure her own mess wasn't making her mom's life difficult.

"No, but they called for an interview the other day. Don't worry, I told them I wasn't interested in making a spectacle of my only daughter."

Walking arm in arm with her, Amber tipped her head to rest against her mother's.

She would never stop loving her no matter what, but there were so many secrets it felt as though they were keeping her from understanding her life, her world. Why would Gloria hide something this big? If Amber ever found out the truth, would she regret it? Would it cause her to think less of her mother? Or would it bring them closer, forging a bond nothing could ever break?

"I'm thinking of changing jobs," Amber said suddenly.

"Why? I thought you liked the freedom?"

"I do, but it's the same-old, same-old. I don't know. Maybe I just need more side projects or something to help with this antsy feeling. I like being able to do things like help Leif with his recipe forums, but I'm having trouble staying motivated with the usual stuff."

"Maybe you just need a boyfriend," Gloria suggested slyly.

Amber let out a burst of laughter. "Because the last one worked out so well for me?"

"Russell doesn't count. You need a nice man who will treat you right. Maybe one from town?"

"And be stuck here forever? No, thanks."

"What's wrong with staying here?"

"Nothing. I just…" The town was home and always had been. But it felt as though there were fewer options to live a life that was more than the same old routine.

"There will come a time when you'll appreciate the quiet, reliable, and predictable. A town that will have your back no matter what."

Amber tried to look at her mother with fresh eyes, not as someone she'd known all her life. She wondered if there had been a time when her mom had needed the town to have her back, and if so, what had happened.

"Like now," Gloria added.

Oh, she was talking about *her*. Right. Amber supposed the town was looking out for her in its usual nosy sort of way. Honestly though, she'd prefer the anonymity of the city when it came to things like this.

"Have you been okay, Mom? With everything?"

"I wish Russell had been a whole lot nicer to you. Someone needs to have a good long talk with his mother."

Amber let out a chuckle. She doubted talking with Mrs. Peaks would change the man's behavior.

They had reached her mother's house, and Gloria let them in, dropping her keys in a dish by the door. She sat on a folding chair, slipping off her shoes so she could massage the balls of her feet, just as she'd done after every shift while Amber was growing up.

"Why didn't you become a stylist after hairdressing school?"

Her mother's thumbs stopped working circles into her soles as she glanced up.

"Hairdressing wasn't for me," she said simply.

"How come?"

She gave a shrug, placing her foot back on the floor. "It just wasn't."

So much for being able to see hidden meanings in her mother's expression. Gloria was as good at poker faces as Scott was.

Either that or there really was nothing behind the hairdressing school rumor.

Her mother went silent, hooking a thumb under her chin, pondering something. "Mary Alice's incident got me thinking. There are things I want you to know, now that you're an adult."

"What incident? What things?" Amber struggled to catch up with this new line of conversation. They were close to something. She could feel it.

"Her lump."

Mary Alice had believed she was dying a few months ago, and

had begun writing relatives' names on pieces of tape, sticking them on various items around her home so they could be handed down after she was gone--much to her husband's consternation. It turned out she'd had just a small malignant tumor that had been safely removed. She was fine now, but that period of not knowing and assuming the worst had been unsettling for more than just Mary Alice. John had said he'd had a run on residents wanting to update their last wills and testaments, and it seemed as though Gloria had been affected, too.

"If you have sex toys or raunchy magazines, you can just go ahead and dispose of those before I have to deal with them."

Her mother breathed heavily through her nose. "Amber, be serious. You've been asking about your family history. Do you want to know or not?"

"Yes, sorry." Now she was worried that Gloria was sick and there were some bad genes kicking around that knocked Thompsons off prematurely. That and what secrets her mother might reveal. Suddenly Amber didn't feel ready.

"I've been thinking about telling you this for some time. I don't know if it's a great time for you, given everything going on with Russell, but either way, you're an adult now and I think you deserve to know."

Amber had to remind herself to breathe, to not blurt out something stupid. Something big was coming down the secrets pipe. Bigger than the name of her father.

"But please know that what I'm about to tell you is confidential. Only four other people know and two of them are dead."

"Um, is this an issue of national security?"

So much for being able to keep her mouth shut, but this was feeling really, really heavy.

Her mother gave her a stern look. "Your grandparents, Amber. Don't be ridiculous. And the secret didn't kill them."

"Sorry. It just sounded like a line from a movie, not our life. I'll shut up and listen. I promise."

"I didn't go to hairdressing school."

"Okay."

"I… I got pregnant in high school."

Her mother had been in her early twenties when she'd had Amber. Which meant… secret baby.

Holy poop. Secret baby!

"I gave her up for adoption."

Amber hadn't seen that one coming. She needed to sit down.

She had a sister. She *was* a sister. To someone. Somewhere. To someone she hadn't even met. Someone who didn't know she existed, just as Amber hadn't known *she'd* existed until seconds ago.

"I mistook sex for love," her mother said heavily, and Amber struggled to pay attention, her mind still reeling from the shock. "I was a fool. Young. I found out I was pregnant two months before graduation. The baby's father didn't want anything to do with us and your grandparents weren't interested in raising another child. So I went away to hairdressing school."

"But you didn't really go there?" Amber slid down the wall, settling on the floor.

This was huge. Huger than Philip not being her father. Huger than Scott applying out. Huger than Russell's book, even. This was a change-her-life-forever secret. A sister!

She had a sister!

"I didn't go. I applied, showed everyone the acceptance letter, then went and worked in a temp agency in the same city until it was time to deliver."

That explained why her mom had burned Amber's forehead with the curling iron and always sent her to the local salon for anything more than a trim. She hadn't even walked through the doors of beauty school.

But to keep such a massive secret for so long. To keep it from everyone. Did Mary Alice know, or simply just suspect, because she didn't have anything better to do with her time?

"Mary Alice hinted that there might be something about you and hairdressing school. Does she know?"

Gloria paused, her face pale, then shook her head. "But if anyone is going to figure out discrepancies in my history, it would be Mary Alice. Not much gets by her."

"But she said…"

"She was probably just fishing, as usual. You've got everyone wondering who your father is, so I'm not surprised she's sifting through my past, looking for hints."

"Oh, Mom. I'm so sorry." Amber hadn't had a clue that there were more secrets that could be exposed by her searching for her father. Her mother had been right when she'd said it was complicated. Getting to the bottom of one secret was like trying to pull a pair of jeans from beneath a towering stack, one-handed, without toppling the others.

"No, no. It's my fault." Gloria let out a long sigh.

"Nobody knows." They sat in silence for a few moments, then Amber tested the words that had been whirling in her head. "I'm a sister."

More silence.

"Where is she?"

"I don't know. I know nothing about her."

"But you could find her, right?"

Gloria shrugged.

"Have you thought about it? Do you want to?"

Her mother let out a shaky sigh laden with sorrow. "She has a family. She doesn't need me interfering and disturbing her life just because I'm curious."

"But what if she's curious, too? What if she wants to know where she came from?"

"She came from the family that adopted her. I gave up my rights."

They were quiet for a long moment.

"Do you regret it?"

"What choice did I have, Amber? I couldn't raise her on my own." Gloria got to her feet, flinging her jacket onto the chair. Then she carefully picked it up and hung it in the closet. "I'm sorry."

"For what?"

"For... everything." She blinked rapidly, sucking in a big breath.

Amber grabbed her in a bear hug, holding her close. She couldn't begin to imagine what her mother must have gone through and the emotions she must have faced--still faced. If Amber was feeling overwhelmed by it all, she couldn't even imagine what her mom must be feeling.

She loosened her grip on her. "Do my sister and I have the same father?"

"No."

Wow. Talk about being unlucky in love. Two daughters and no fathers for either of them. Maybe Amber didn't need to find her dad to understand why things hadn't worked out with her and Russell. Maybe it was a maternal bad-luck-in-love gene--one that kicked in once they stopped believing in themselves and their power to determine their own futures. *Boom! Here's your bad luck, ma'am.*

But how had these secrets not burned up her mother? To have two children out of wedlock. To give one away. To be rejected by two baby daddies. So many secrets. So much sorrow.

Maybe Thompson women were stronger than they thought.

"Can we find her?"

"Oh, I don't know, Amber."

Amber needed to know what her sister was like--what she herself might be capable of achieving. Would finding her missing sibling show her mother that she didn't need to keep her secrets any longer? People traced long-lost family members all the time.

It had been well over twenty years ago and nobody would judge a teen mom for something like that now. Nobody was perfect, and as Scott said, everyone had secrets. So why not own up and move past it? Bury the sorrow under love and discovery? Stop wondering and regretting and start living.

And at the end of the day, maybe her father wasn't who Amber needed to meet to figure herself out, maybe it was her sister. And maybe, just maybe, finding her would help set their mom free, as well.

<hr>

AMBER'S MOTHER hadn't said yes, but she hadn't said no when Amber asked if they could find her sister. She'd simply asked Amber to let things sink in first.

Well, things had sunk in and Amber was excited and hopeful. There was no way she couldn't try to find her. What if she had nieces and nephews? What if she and her sister had tons in common? She couldn't resist trying to find out.

She wouldn't tell a soul. She could keep it a secret. She wouldn't betray her mother's trust and confidence.

She could do this. And it was so easy. There were piles of websites and forums where adopted children were seeking their biological parents or siblings, and vice versa. Some sites allowed her to type in birth dates to narrow down the search--even though all she had was the year, a possible January birth, the fact that it was a baby girl, and the city she had been born in. But so far Amber had found four possible matches.

As a precaution, she'd added her name to the government's application system--a sibling searching sibling. She'd had to mail information and documents proving her identity but it would take them several weeks to confirm who she was, as well as search for any possible matches in their system. But that was easy, too. And if her sister had granted permission for family members to contact her, then Amber would have something. Otherwise, her name and information would remain in the database until her sister added herself--if ever.

Amber decided if she got as far as finding her, and had contact information, she would discuss the search with her mother. At that point, she figured, Gloria wouldn't be able to resist meeting her long-lost baby girl.

With a renewed desire to get to the bottom of the secrets surrounding her, Amber sent messages to the four possible matches on the nongovernment website. While it was a discouragingly small number, with no obvious feeling of "this must be her," at least it wasn't thousands of people she had to sift through with her limited information.

Amber's phone rang as she hit "Send" on the last message. It was Liz, calling as John Abcott's receptionist, requesting a meeting in the lawyer's office ASAP.

That couldn't be good.

What did Russell want now?

AMBER SAT across from the lawyer, wondering why he'd called her into his office. Did John know about how to track down her sister, and want to help? No, that was a silly idea. He knew nothing about Gloria's secret baby. Amber was suspecting secrets where there couldn't be ones now.

He tapped his fingers on the table he used as a desk and cleared his throat, then adjusted his reading glasses on his nose. "How are you doing with everything that's going on?"

"Okay." Amber had poured herself a coffee from the pot near Liz's reception desk, and turned the cup around in her hands. The liquid was so dark she was afraid to drink it; even with cream and sugar added it had a lethal look to it. "You still have the old soccer team photos in your reception area."

John had coached her soccer team all through the years, as well as sponsored jerseys and fees through his office. He'd been on parent council and organized all sorts of other things for kids in the community. How the man ever found the time was beyond her.

"I do," he said, taking a sip from the water glass to his right. "How's your mom doing?"

"Fine."

John was a lunch regular at Benny's, which was a mere block away. If anyone knew how Gloria was doing, it was likely customers such as John.

"Good. She always wanted to travel, and now that you're all grown up I keep imagining her just up and taking off one day." Her mother wanted to travel? How many secrets did that woman have? "I'm actually heading out on a trip next week, which is what made me think about it."

"That's nice." Amber checked her watch. Usually the two of them sat along the bar in Brew Babies, shooting the breeze and sharing several bowls of nuts, as well as a few vodka shots, but she really didn't have time today. "I don't mean to be rude, but I have a conference call for work in half an hour. Sorry to hurry things along, but what did you need me for?"

"Right. I'm sorry. Russell contacted me about his holiday trailer." John passed a piece of paper to Amber. "He wants you to pay the amount owed, and plans to take you to court if you don't cover it. Consider this letter a shot across the proverbial bow--a warning."

She twined her fingers together, elbows resting on the chair's armrests. "Right. That's not happening."

John was like Scott--respected, knew everyone. A man who could be relied on. He was also someone she could be a straight with.

His eyebrows rose incrementally as he leaned forward, echoing her pose. "How so?"

"He put my life in a book. You know, tit for tat. Even if it was an accidental dose of tit."

"That just sounds wrong," John said with a chuckle.

Amber made a face and John stood, turning to lift a decorative box that sat behind him. He revealed a single-cup coffeemaker and a bottle of vodka. "Name your poison."

"Coffee, please." She had to work later.

She looked at the sludge in her cup, realizing she was ordering what she already had.

John said quickly, "Don't drink that."

He began measuring coffee and water into the machine, before switching it on and returning to his seat. "Do you think you have a case for libel?"

"Did you read the book? Everyone knows I'm Ember, even though he keeps saying I'm not. He called Scott Sir Studly, and now everyone thinks I'm in love with him. Well, Liz and Mary Alice, anyway." Maybe not the strongest argument to bring to a small-town lawyer.

"Were you financially supporting him while he wrote the book?"

"He was on paid sabbatical." She slumped deeper into the chair. "He took things that I said..." She paused, trying to control the emotions that were ravaging her vocal cords and making it impossible for her to speak clearly. "He took me out of context. It's my life. I should have a right to have things we said remain private. I'm not a public persona."

"Real people are used as inspiration all the time. He was within the bounds of the law by the sounds of things--sorry, I haven't read the book yet. But from what I understand, he changed your name, age, career, locale, and therefore used nothing considered identifying information. People always think they know the characters in an author's book. Especially if they know the author well."

"He named the main character *Ember*." Amber held up a

finger. "That is one letter off of my name. Doesn't that say it all? And didn't he have insurance on his little writing cave? Because that was totally an accident. I filed a report with Scott and everything."

"No insurance. And he claims it was intentional, vindictive destruction of his personal property." John propped his fingers in a steeple, then removed his reading glasses. "I should warn you that keeping a low profile during the next few months would be wise. The press could have a field day with your personal life if these allegations become widely known."

She bowed her head, thinking of her mother. Amber would love to go after Russell for defaming her, but if she was going to protect her mom, her secrets, and sort out her own problems, she was going to have to give up battling her ex.

"I'd like to make a counter offer if I could."

"Sure." John picked up his pen. "What do you have in mind?"

"He drops the idea that I need to pay for the trailer and I won't sue him for libel."

"He's the type that would like you suing him--all publicity is good publicity, and publicity sells more books."

Amber sighed. She didn't feel it was right to have to pay for his trailer. Not when he had wronged her in so many different ways. She needed something to make him go away. Something good.

"Don't reply yet then," she said. "I might come up with something."

John swung his chair around to retrieve her cup of coffee, doctored it with just the right amount of cream and sugar, and placed it in front of her, taking away the cruddy cup she'd previously ignored.

How did he know how she took her coffee?

"I heard you're looking for your father?"

Amber started, her attention jerking from her java to the man seated across from her.

He wasn't her father, she reminded herself. He just knew what everyone else in town knew. Or maybe a bit more, if she was lucky.

"Do you know who my mom was dating just before Philip?" Her heart was beating so fast and hard that in her peripheral vision she swore could see it moving her shirt.

"Which time?"

"She dated him more than once?"

John nodded.

Why would they get back together? Because Gloria was pregnant and she thought Philip might be the father? Or she was pregnant by someone else and Philip thought he'd try to help, but then bailed? Or he'd found out after they were back together that the baby wasn't his?

So many questions. One big secret.

"The time my mom got pregnant with me." Amber gripped her cup of coffee so hard she feared she was going to break the handle. "Who did she date before Philip Powers?"

"Me."

AMBER HAD HIGHTAILED it out of John's office, just about getting run over crossing the street, she'd been moving so fast, completely freaked out by John's revelation.

He was her father?

There was no way.

No. Way.

In terms of dads, he was well out of her league. He was steady, strong, smart, confident, and more.

Then again, he'd been divorced twice, and it wasn't as though she was faring particularly well in the dating world. However, she could already lay the blame for that on her mother's side of the family.

But a man like him still couldn't be her dad. He'd practically received Father of the Year for the way he'd raised his daughter, Marisa, as well as half the kids in the community. Men like that didn't beget children like Amber, who could barely keep her life together and dated all the wrong guys, hoping against hope that things would lead to a happily ever after.

That moment in John's office though… she hadn't known what to do other than panic and flee. But back in the safety of her house she realized she had to be mistaken. As in way wrong. She'd completely misinterpreted what he'd said. He'd dated her mother before she'd hooked up with Philip. Big deal. Amber remembered someone mentioning that ages ago. Gloria had also dated Mandy's uncle and nobody thought he was Amber's father.

If John was, people in town would have known. *She* would know. There had to be a mystery man. A mysterious figure John must know something about if he was bringing up the subject. And she'd blown it by running out.

The poor man was probably sitting in his office right now wondering what had scared her off, or else was trying to correlate Amber's birthday with the last time he'd been with Gloria.

Thank goodness Amber hadn't said anything. *That* would have been embarrassing.

She puttered around the house, having managed to stumble her way through her conference call despite her distraction.

Someone knocked on the front door, and she peered out the upstairs window as her mom called out, "Anyone home?"

"Up here!" Amber scrambled down the stairs to greet her. They hadn't talked since the sister revelation. She hoped her mother had come to say they should look for her.

"I heard you talked to John today," Gloria said with no preamble.

"I did." Amber smoothed her shirt. "Russell didn't have insurance and wants me to pay for his trailer."

Her mother picked a USB cable off the kitchen counter, coiled it, and set it down, moving on to straighten and tidy other objects Amber had left out.

"He said he may have upset you while talking about your father."

"He said you two dated."

"We did. You knew that."

"I'd forgotten."

"What else did he say?"

"About my dad?" There was something off about her mother's behavior, and Amber wondered once again how much John knew. "Nothing."

Gloria watched her carefully. Then, seemingly satisfied, she gave a short nod, her shoulders relaxing.

Yep. John definitely knew something.

"Can you tell me something about my dad? I promise I won't tell anyone."

"Amber, it's complicated." Her mother was using her exasperated voice.

"I know."

How could she convince Gloria it was safe to open up to her? So many secrets had been revealed, and yet nothing had come from any of them. Amber was no closer to understanding herself and no closer to resolving her past. Having the unknown just out of reach was driving her to distraction.

"Amber, you can't… I never asked him to help."

"Why not? Why didn't he step up, anyway?"

"I didn't ask him to because I was embarrassed. He's successful. Wonderful. And I had gotten myself pregnant again and should have known better."

They had sat down at the kitchen table and Amber cupped her hand over her mother's in support. "It takes two to tango, Mom."

She could tell that her father had seared a tattoo on her

mother's heart, and despite everything, she still carried a torch for him. How could that even be possible?

"He's a family man now, just not my family man," her mother said softly, and Amber could hear the sorrow and longing in her voice. She'd had cared enough to keep track of him.

But what kind of man went off to raise his own family and ignored Gloria's? Sure, it happened to plenty of women, but still. This was *her* mother.

Wait. He was a family man. That meant Amber had half siblings.

In the period of a few days she had gone from an only child to having several siblings. It was a good thing she was sitting down already, otherwise she would probably have needed a chair.

As a teen she'd half wondered whether Philip had gone on to have more kids, but it hadn't felt real. Not like this.

She was a sister several times over. And she had no clue who her siblings were or if they even knew of her existence. What if one of her friends was actually related to her?

No, couldn't be. Her father wasn't from town.

"He didn't need some waitress coming to him about love children."

"Wait!" Amber held up her hand, trying to guess the meaning of her mother's words. "Wait. He doesn't *know?*"

"Why would I come forward after all these years? I'm nothing special. Just a chubby, washed-up, middle-aged woman who never amounted to anything. I never even got out of this town to go see the world."

See the world.

John *had* known her mother well. And he definitely knew more than Amber had realized.

"You're an amazing woman and not just *some waitress,*" Amber said, trying to console her mom, wanting her to know that she thought the world of her. And yet her mind was still stuck on the idea that her father didn't know who she was.

"You can memorize twenty-five orders. That's more than just 'some waitress'." Amazed as a child at how her mother could balance loaded plates all the way up her arm, and cup three water glasses in the palm of one hand, Amber had brought all the kids she could find into Benny's to show off her and her skills. Back then being a waitress had seemed glamorous, not a job for someone with no other options.

"Amber, you all ordered Orange Crush and French fries, except for Devon, who ordered root beer. It was hardly a challenge."

"Oh."

"That's all nine-year-olds order if given a choice." Gloria propped her head in her hands and Amber found herself echoing the pose.

"So, he doesn't know who I am? That I exist?" she confirmed.

Her mother nodded sadly.

Amber was stunned. How could her father not have figured out that he had a child? He had to be an out-of-towner. Had to be.

She sat back, sorting through her feelings. Part of her felt relieved. She hadn't been rejected by her dad, because if he didn't know about her, he couldn't reject her. It hadn't even been a case of her mother not being enough to keep her man.

She felt buoyant and as though she had been freed. The knowledge opened up a whole new avenue of beliefs. Her father could be delighted to have her, and would welcome her into his arms and his family. He might claim her as his, as one of his clan.

"He tried to talk to me about it once and I implied that you weren't his."

"But why?"

"He had his own family by then. A wife. A kid on the way. He was starting a business and didn't need the conflict."

"Conflict?" Was that what she was? A conflict to be avoided?

An obligation best not undertaken? Amber was so insulted she wanted to leave, but it was her house.

"We'd been dating in secret."

Not more secrets. Would they never end? She was getting *so* tired of secrets. So tired of being five steps behind her own life. Amber fought for patience, fought to keep her mouth shut so she didn't ask her mom what she'd been thinking, dating a guy like that. When Amber found true love she wanted her man to be strong enough to tell everyone she was his. To claim her despite anyone else's misgivings.

"His parents didn't approve and thought he should marry someone else. So we started dating in secret, trying to sort out who we were without interference from his family. He was my one. I loved him like no other."

Her mother fell silent.

"And?"

"I wanted him to know everything about me. I told him about your sister and we broke up." Gloria paused and looked at Amber. "I can see what you're thinking, and it wasn't like that. It was my idea to keep it secret. He needed his family's support for what he was doing, but in the end I wasn't enough. What I'd done… I think it confirmed everything his family had been saying about me. But I had to be honest with him, Amber. I couldn't keep it a secret. Not from him. I wanted to marry him. I just wish he could have… I wish we…" She grew silent again.

"He broke up with you because you wanted a better life for my sister? Didn't he see what your mom and dad were like?" What kind of jerk would judge her mother for doing what she felt was best? The only person who had been hurt was Gloria. Amber wanted to meet this man and give him a good shake for not seeing that Amber's grandmother, who had worked in a bingo parlor, and grandfather, who had packed up and left long before that, were hardly supportive parents. Gloria would have been a seventeen-year-old trying to raise a baby on her own. Even Amber could see that.

"He came from a different world, a different kind of family. He didn't understand why I did what I did, and I felt so weak and selfish that I couldn't stand up for myself and own it. I was devastated by his judgment. I had thought I'd made the right choice. We had a massive fight and out of spite I got back together with my ex."

"Philip."

Her mother nodded.

"But nobody knows who this man is, because you were dating in secret?"

She nodded again.

Amber thought back to what her mother had said about giving up her first child. "Do you regret putting my sister up for adoption?"

"It wouldn't have been easy, keeping her, but I would have two wonderful daughters right now, wouldn't I? I wouldn't have the burden of all this." Gloria's voice was wobbling with indignant anger. "And maybe if I had kept her I could have shown him, shown the world, that I was more than just a woman who screwed up. I was a woman who persevered and…" She sighed deeply. "Oh, I don't know. Just… something."

They sat in silence for a moment.

This was Amber's opening. Her chance to tell her mom that she had begun the search for her sister. Her heart thundered in her chest. She had a temporary secret from her mother, but was terrified to reveal it.

"Do you want to meet her?" she asked, her voice barely above a whisper.

Gloria rubbed her eyes with the tips of her fingers. "I don't know, Amber. I don't think I could handle it if she was mad at me. It was such a big sacrifice--for both of us. She might not understand my decision."

"You wanted the best life for my sister and you made the appropriate arrangements in order to ensure it. Nobody can fault that. Nobody worthy of your time, anyway."

Her mother gave her a sad smile, gently patting her cheek. "I'm tired. I'm going to head home and call it a night. I'm sorry I've kept so many secrets from you. I hope you're not mad and that you can forgive me."

"There's nothing to forgive," Amber said in surprise. "And I'm not mad. I'm just confused." Torn up. Baffled by how things had progressed in her mother's world, to the point where she felt too ashamed to tell the man she loved that he was a father. Amber wanted to understand, but felt a lot of anger at the injustice of his actions.

Her throat tightened as she thought about how her mother had felt forced to make such a heartbreaking choice alone--for a second time. What if Amber had been born first? What would her life have been like? She couldn't imagine not having her mom, her rock, in her life.

"Why did you decide to keep me?" she asked.

"Oh, Amber." Her mother's eyes filled with tears. "There is no way I could have made that same decision a second time." She held both of Amber's hands in her own. "I'm stronger now than I was then, and it's not fair of me to think I'd do anything differently if I went back in time, but I still do. Learn from my mistakes, Amber. Believe you're enough woman for Scott. He loves you and sometimes love *is* enough. Trust your heart."

Amber rolled her eyes. One silly novel and everyone suddenly thought she was in love with her best friend, Sir Studly. Sure, he was a great man who would make a wonderful boyfriend or husband, but that didn't mean she was secretly wishing she could be his.

"Scott may still be harboring a crush from when we were kids, but it's nothing real. He would never love me in the way I would want him to. If, in theory, I decided to fall in love with him."

"Deciding who to fall in love with is like deciding where and when lightning is going to strike. You don't get to choose those things. Scott loves you just the way you are--goofy and quicker to act than think--and he always has. You just need to believe that you're enough for him."

"Mom..." Amber warned.

"You know what?" Gloria perked up suddenly. "That's good advice. What about me? Isn't it my time? Shouldn't I start believing in myself, too?"

Okay, now her mother was taking a dive off the deep end without a life jacket.

"I think it's high time I became the woman I always wanted to be."

"What does that mean?" Amber asked.

"I'll call you!" she said, hurrying to the door.

"About what?

Gloria continued on.

"Are you going to tell my dad about me?" Amber asked hopefully.

Her mom popped her head back into the room. "Ha, ha. No."

"Then what?"

"I have to see how much money I have in my tip jar."

Great. Her mother was going to skip town, and now Amber would never learn the truth about anything.

4

Amber sat in Brew Babies, twirling a vodka shot the bartender, Moe, had placed in front of her when she'd sat down. She couldn't help but think how alike she and her mother seemed to be when it came to screwing up their lives around men. How had her mom's life come to this? All those secrets and regrets. Was Amber's life going to devolve into that, too?

"Not going to drink?" Moe asked.

She didn't mind a shot here or there, but today her mind was already a mess and she was afraid of what she might say if vodka loosened her tongue.

"Maybe not today." She passed the shot over to Moe, who shrugged and knocked it back himself.

"No point wasting it," he said.

"Do you have any chocolate?" she asked.

"Chocolate martini."

Amber considered it. Alcohol had been unfriended for the moment. "I was thinking chocolate drops. Didn't you have some in wineglasses the other week?"

"It was part of Mandy's engagement party. Katie decorated for us."

"Oh, right." Her friend had decided to give up nursing and go into interior decorating. She came home every once in awhile to add flourishes to people's events. "Any leftovers?"

Moe smiled and pulled a coffee cup from under the bar, setting it in front of her. She peeked over the rim and saw two chocolate drops in need of rescue.

"Thank you."

He continued down the bar, serving up several pints of the pub's home brews.

Amber sat thinking as the first chocolate drop melted in her mouth. She was already feeling more human, her mind settling down to a gentle hum instead of three different heavy metal radio stations playing at once.

Moe returned a moment later. "Are you applying for Amy's job? I'll put a good word in for you."

"I have a job." Amy, the pub's main waitress, was a rolling stone who had come back to waitressing time and again, even after trying other careers. Amber didn't doubt that the woman would go back to waitressing again in six months to a year--after her latest adventure. It was as though once you served a burger in Blueberry Springs you became a lifer and couldn't give it up. Look at her mom, and even Mandy, who'd opened her own restaurant but still served customers just like when she'd been a waitress. Only now she was a boss.

"I heard you lost your job."

"I didn't lose my job!"

"Oh."

"And even if I had, there are other things I could do besides waitressing."

"I guess I just thought because your mom does it, you would, too."

"We're different people." Amber stood, gathering her purse.

They *were* different people, right? She wasn't going to follow in her mother's footsteps. She was going to find love. She was going to have a family. A big one. All together. With no secrets other than what they'd bought each other for Christmas.

"I didn't mean anything by it. You've just got a great way with people, an excellent memory. You'd make great tips, like your mom."

"Right. Of course." Amber gave a smile and wove her way between tables, heading toward the large doors that would spit her out onto the sidewalk. But when she saw Mandy with an empty chair beside her, she plopped down before realizing her friend was actually in the middle of what looked to be a business meeting. The woman with her was done up to the hilt, and dripping in jewelry as though she was a tree in a rainforest, covered in hanging moss.

"You must be Amber Thompson," the woman said, before Amber could apologize for the interruption and move along.

"Yes, sorry. I didn't mean to disturb your meeting," she said, standing again.

"Not at all," said Mandy, perking up. "Actually, you know how to make computers go, right?"

Amber tried to hold in a sigh. What was it with everyone thinking that her database job meant she was a techie? "I work with databases. Whatever your computer problem, you probably just have to turn it off and on again. Think of snarky computers as a man who's in a mood. Reset his processor to make him more cooperative."

"I need spreadsheet, database stuff," Mandy said. "I'm up to my eyeballs in paper and need to implement some serious efficiencies."

"I can totally help with that if you pay me in brownies."

"Deal," Mandy said, with a relieved ghost of a smile. Her friend was seriously working too hard again.

The woman with Mandy extended her hand, a slight smile

that looked a lot like respect and amusement tweaking her perfectly colored lips. "Blair Diggs. I'm one of the restaurant chain owners Mandy works with."

"Pleased to meet you. I interrupted--I'm sorry."

"I'm not." Blair leaned forward, one hand on Amber's arm, preventing her from making an escape. "I heard what you did to Russell Peaks and I have to admit it's even better than what I did to him."

"I'm sorry—what?" Amber had lowered her voice and immediately searched the pub for eavesdroppers. She spotted Scott standing in the doorway, talking into the walkie-talkie clipped to his lapel, and laughing. His jaw looking as sharp and angular as his broad shoulders.

"Smashing his writing office?" Blair said. "Good on you. It's about time someone hit him where it hurts. Again."

"You dated Russell?" Mandy exclaimed, her eyes round.

"Where did you hit him?" Amber asked.

"In the leg."

"With what?" Mandy demanded.

"A bullet."

Amber glanced over her shoulder, on the lookout for Scott, who seemed to have left the building. She was starting to wish she'd taken Moe up on that shot.

"Sadly, not the middle leg?" she asked.

Blair rewarded her joke with a deep chuckle. "No, not that one. My aim was off."

"He said he got shot getting a story," Amber stated, her voice low. Was Blair yanking her chain? Russell wasn't a faultless prince, but she'd seen the awards on his wall.

"He lied," Blair said simply, flipping her hand palm up as if the untruth didn't bother her in the least.

"Why?" Mandy asked, leaning forward. She inched her chair closer, then swept her long mane of blond hair off her shoulders. "Why did you do it?"

"He cheated on me. Used me."

Amber mulled that over. Russell was probably already cheating on his editor. She had a pretty good feeling he was using Sabrina to try and get his book the best shot at the charts. Amber was certain she hadn't been the first woman Russell had hooked up with in anticipation of his next career move and what she could provide. Which left her wondering where Blair fit in. What was her piece in the Russell puzzle?

"What did he want you for?" Amber asked. Blair's eyebrows shot up in surprise. "I mean, he dated me because he wanted my story--even though it's not me in the book. No, really," she told Mandy, who gave her a "yeah, right" look. "Then when he had the story he cheated on me with his editor, because he wanted the book to get the best chance at making it. He's probably already lining up his next victim to help him with his next plan. So? What did he use you for?"

Blair sat back, arms crossed, assessing Amber. "You're shrewd. I like that. You've pushed the emotional stuff aside and are already moving forward. Very business minded. Do you run your own company?"

"No."

"You should. You'd be good at it." Blair took a sip of her wine. "Me? I fell for Russell's song and dance."

"It's a pretty good song," Amber admitted.

"But in the end, I was the one shooting at *his* feet, making that chicken dance to a whole new beat."

The women sat silently for a moment and Amber and Mandy shared a look. Amber would bet Mandy was currently reconsidering any plans that might upset Blair.

"I was married to the TV station's owner at the time," Blair said, her manicured finger idly tracing the rim of her wineglass until the glass started to sing.

"You had an affair? Last time I ask you for relationship advice," Mandy grumbled.

"Oh, I have all the advice because I've made all the mistakes. Keep asking, sugar."

"And so?" Amber pressed, eager for details.

"And so I made a fool of myself. I got Russell his promotion and he turned my life upside down. I didn't like being used or lied to, so I met up with him in whatever forsaken country he was in. It was so hot and dry. Hard on the skin, I remember that. Anyway, long story made very short--I shot him. And he turned it into a tale of bravery." She let out a bitter laugh.

Amber thought about Blair's story for a moment. Both of them had been cheated on. Which meant Amber had likely been "the other woman" for someone Russell had dated between her and Blair.

Amber stood. "Pleasure to have met you." She turned to her friend. "Watch out for this one. She knows how to aim a gun."

Mandy choked on her drink, shooting Blair a worried look as the woman leaned over to pat her on the back.

Amber headed for the door, seeking a quiet place where she could pause and think about Russell and his get-ahead strategies. There was something she could use from that conversation. She was sure of it.

A hand reached out and grabbed her by the arm as she passed the second last table between her and solitude. It was Wanda, who ran the bridal store in town, sitting with Liz.

Gossips.

"I heard you're looking for your father," Wanda said, still gripping her as though Amber was in danger of running away.

Smart lady.

"I am." Amber hunched down so she could lower her voice and avoid others overhearing them. "Do you know who he is?"

Both women shook their heads.

"Well, if you find out, tell him I don't like him." Amber straightened, ready to make her exit.

The women gasped, asking about fifty questions at once as

Amber turned, almost slamming into Scott. She placed her hands against his chest, sparks zipping up her arms as she made contact. He smelled like heaven and looked as fit and manly as ever in his police uniform.

He gallantly touched the brim of his hat. "Ladies." He looked at Amber in a way that made her "Hey, Scott," come out all breathy.

She needed to school her brain. He was her best friend. Just because everyone thought they should be together and they'd almost-kissed on Valentine's Day didn't mean she should start swooning. It was ridiculous. Utterly.

The two women made room for Scott at their table.

"Sorry, ladies. On duty, but another time."

"Amber was just telling us she doesn't like her father."

Scott glanced at Amber, who gave a small shake of her head.

The jukebox began playing Adele's "Make You Feel My Love" and Amber cringed. It had been her and Russell's song. Why had he bothered going through all the motions of a relationship if he didn't care and had only been using her? Had any of it been real? She had a feeling that for men like Russell it was always just a game.

"Amber, may I have this dance?" Scott asked, already ushering her away from the ladies.

"I don't dance." The last thing she wanted to do was dance to this stupid song with a man who made her feel as if… as if love might actually be possible one day.

"You look like you're going to rip someone's head off, so just shut up and let me distract you. Telling those ladies stuff about how you're feeling is not going to go well for you in the long run." He placed a palm on her hip, holding out his left hand, waiting for her to take it. She stepped into his shadow, the heat radiating from his body wrapping around her, his touch sending shock waves of longing through her.

So much for schooling her brain. It was running through the

gutters, splashing and yelling "Yippee!" as it daydreamed of all the things her body could do with this hunk of male specimen cozied up against her.

"Besides, you danced with me in February." Scott's lips curved into a slow smile, his tone teasing.

Yeah, they'd danced. And then she'd almost kissed him. Kind of like what she wanted to do right now.

Which was silly. Kissing her best friend would just make things messy and complicated.

Scott two-stepped them onto the empty dance floor and the heat of his hand began to leach through her light sweater, making her aware of how close he was. She lost track of where her feet were supposed to be and nearly fell into Mandy's table, but Scott caught her, swooping her up as though she'd meant to do a grand dip. He handled her with care, making her feel as though she was graceful. She wanted him to do it again. And again.

Naked.

Okay, she really needed to get out more. She was lusting after Scott in ways that twisted her brain.

"When are you two going to kiss?" called Wanda over the music.

Great, she saw it, too. In fact, the whole quiet pub probably did seeing as they were the only two dancing.

"She's going back to the city. They're not going to kiss," Liz grumbled.

"Scott's leaving, too," Wanda pointed out.

"Ladies, enough," he said. "Just because it was their song doesn't mean I can't dance with her." He gave them a look as though to say, "How do you think she feels?" His tone was light, authoritative and protective, making Amber struggle with the desire to rest her head against his shoulder and never let go.

"Thank you," she whispered. "But don't you think it's better to just ignore them?"

Scott studied her for a long moment. "Ignoring problems doesn't work."

"Fighting gossip just fuels it." She ran her hand over his shoulder, taking in its size.

"Were you finally going to come to the city with me?" she asked, referring to Wanda's earlier comment about him leaving. He'd possibly assumed, rightly, that as soon as Russell broke up with her she'd take off again. But so far, she hadn't quite gotten there.

Too many things to clear up first.

Scott slowed their dancing as a call came through over the walkie-talkie clipped to his lapel.

Her hand drifted down to his name tag, tracing the letters over his breast pocket. She loved that even now he held her tight and wouldn't let her drift away. She should stop touching him, stop enjoying his attention and how good it felt dancing with him, but couldn't seem to force herself to let go. He was definitely going to get the wrong idea.

"Sorry. I've got to check this out," he said, after getting a code through his walkie-talkie. He released her, leaving her feeling abandoned and cold. As he backed off, he pointed at her in a way that pinned her to the spot. "You still owe me a dance if I don't come back."

"Yeah," she said weakly. "Any time."

Her mind was fuzzy and her body was sending messages that were definitely earmarked for the beyond-friends forbidden zone. She needed to get her life together. She needed to overcome the hopeless feeling that she would never have true love with a man as wonderful as Scott. The despair that needled her was causing her to take notice of any men who were 100% all male--such as him. She looked toward the bar, where Moe was drying a glass. He was cute. Maybe she could latch her lusty need onto him.

Problem was, he wasn't doing a thing for her.

There was just something so right about Scott. Every inch of her body that he'd brushed or touched during their impromptu dance was burning, waiting to feel him again. Their history and his gentle kindness were making him an easy target for her melted mind. Right now, the way she was feeling, if the man had had groupies following him every time he was in uniform it wouldn't have surprised her. In fact, she'd ask to join the club.

He was going to make some woman lucky someday. Very lucky. But until he found someone she was going to take advantage of his attention.

———

HER MOTHER HAD LEFT. Signed up for a cruise and taken off, just like that. And it wasn't the fancy cars show 'n' shine, cruise around town that Frankie Smith and his parts store buddies had planned again for this June. It was off to see the world on a giant ship. Alone. Immediately.

Amber didn't like it. Her mother knew Amber needed answers and yet she'd run off for ten days in hopes of finding herself.

It didn't help that Amber already had two emails back from possible siblings saying they'd already found their families. The emails had brought with them a strange mix of anger and sadness that left Amber down in the dumps for days. She couldn't take much more uncertainty. She needed answers.

Although maybe if her mother found herself she would see that she needed to unbury her secrets and spill her guts-- completely. Both to Amber and Amber's father.

But waiting another ten days sounded a lot like torture. Patience was not all that and more, as everyone said. Good things came to people who waited? Yeah, maybe. But even better things came to those who went out and snagged it for themselves. They got a bigger chunk of that pie, not the leftover crumbs that were missing the chocolaty middle goodness.

Great, now she wanted a slice of Benny's chocolate maven pie.

Opening her laptop, Amber checked the job queue to see if there was any work waiting for her, then headed to Benny's in the golf cart. One slice of pie with a tall glass of milk coming up. Being back in Blueberry Springs had definitely been hard on her hips.

She parked out back of Benny's and let herself in through the delivery entrance. "Hey, Benny!" she said as she passed his office on the way to find Leif.

"Oh, I've been meaning to call you today."

"Well, here I am!" she said brightly.

He joined her in the hall, moving out of the way of a waitress heading for the kitchen, and pulled Amber in for a one-armed hug. Was he her dad? He'd always been paternal. Somehow she just couldn't see Benny's family causing interference with his love life. Plus he'd been married for about thirty years and lived in town. Not her father.

"I know I've said this before, but your mother sure is happy to see you home. It's astounding how similar you two are. I don't know many mothers and daughters as close as you. "

Except for the secrets, of course. That was acting a bit like a pry bar at the moment.

"She is a pretty awesome mother."

"Awesome waitress, too. With her finally asking for some holiday time I couldn't say no, although it's left me in a bit of a pinch. I don't suppose you'd consider helping out? I know you have a job and all, but maybe a little extra to help you save up for moving back to the city again? Your mother makes astounding tips."

"Um…" The look on Benny's face was going to do her in. His double chins, his big round eyes pleading like a puppy's.

"Think about it."

The man had been there for her with hugs and food for eons.

"Leif's in the kitchen and I have it on good authority that he just made another batch of pie."

Oh, the pie. She *always* got free pie.

Talk about giving her a ticket to guilt express.

He needed help.

But it was waitressing.

If Amber said yes, she'd effectively become her mother. She'd never get out of town.

She couldn't do it. She'd promised herself. Move upward. Obtain more--all those things her mother hadn't.

Benny gave her chin a gentle chuck, then stepped back toward his office.

But it was just for a few days. Part-time. Helping out a family friend.

She had to do it. She couldn't let Benny down.

"Okay, fine," she said quickly, the pressure getting to her. "I'll do it. Only part-time, though. I still have my full-time job to contend with."

Benny squeezed her in an extra large, cushiony hug. She could handle someone like him being her father. All those pillowy hugs.

He released her, holding her out in front of him. "Thank you."

"Just while she's away."

"She has about six months of holiday time banked."

"What?"

Benny laughed. "Worry not, young one." He tapped the end of her nose. "She's only gone ten days." He headed to his office, triumphant. "This time."

Amber walked slowly to the kitchen, shaking her head. Taking off to travel the world. Her mother was becoming a force to be reckoned with, wasn't she?

Either that or she'd found an easy way to run from Amber and her secrets.

Amber grabbed a slice of pie and a glass of milk from Leif,

sitting in the staff room to eat her snack as she had so many times as a kid. She allowed her mind to wander while she ate.

She dropped her fork suddenly. She had it! The one thing that might cause Russell to back off.

She dialed John's cell phone, leaving a voice mail. "John, it's Amber. I have it. Send Russell my counteroffer asking him to drop the trailer thing. And then let it slip that I was talking to Blair Diggs and she told me an interesting story set in a hot, dry climate."

Amber hung up, smiling. She'd bet anything that Blair's story was legit and that Russell wouldn't want the truth of how he got his limp being leaked, causing him to go from hero to zero in no time flat.

Sure, it was blackmail, and John might not go through with it, but she had nothing to lose.

Her phone binged with an incoming email and she checked it as she finished the last of her milk, just about choking. It was from a woman who thought she might be Amber's long-lost sister.

5

Her mother was seizing the day and chasing after her dreams, and what was Amber up to? Nothing.

The same old, same old.

Well, other than mulling over the new discoveries in her life. Such as her father didn't know of her existence. She had a possible sister who wanted to meet up. She had an undetermined number of half siblings. Her mother was no longer the predictable, staid woman Amber had always counted on. And her ex-boyfriend wanted money for his stupid writing cave.

Oh, and she was daydreaming about her best friend in a friends-to-lovers kind of way.

Her mom had told her to believe she was enough woman for Scott and now Amber couldn't get the idea out of her mind. Or the arguments about how her mother had to be wrong. Scott Malone was a man who upheld laws, whereas Amber went out and stumbled into them, sometimes shattering them in her wake. Her friend hadn't come to the city when she'd left town, despite her constant begging. She hadn't been enough for him to consider uprooting himself. And now that she was here for an indeterminate length of time, he was leaving. She'd never be enough. She got herself into embarrassing situations and it was too much for a man like Scott to take. As a friend, fine. As more? Not happening.

Besides, they weren't even well matched. Not beyond their awesome friendship. For example, Scott definitely wouldn't be considering finding a long-lost sibling without consulting his parents first.

As Amber was.

The email from her possible sister requesting a get together was open on her laptop, staring at her. Amber really wanted to meet the woman named Delia Whitehart. She didn't want to wait for her mother or the government to confirm their relationship. Sick with excitement and fear, Amber wanted to find out everything about Delia. Every single little thing.

They could have a ton in common and become best friends.

Then again, her sister might not want to have anything to do with her after she found out that Amber was the flaky heroine in a new novel currently taking the country by storm.

Amber wanted to be like her mother and seize the day, jump on the offered unicorn of dreams and ride it over the rainbow and into the sunset.

But she couldn't. It would mean not thinking about the impact on her mother.

Being an adult sucked.

Yet she could still argue that this was her sister and it was her right to meet her.

And on the other side of the argument, Amber would be betraying her mother and her trust. But then why would her mom mention her sister if she didn't secretly want Amber to find her?

She felt as though she was standing on the edge of a cliff. The edge of truth. A turning point in her life. Before sister; after sister. If she didn't pursue this, she'd always wonder.

But pursuing it could cause a rift between her and her mother.

Instead of continuing to argue with herself, Amber got in the golf cart and drove into Blueberry Springs, parking in front of the police station. Scott was sitting at his desk, typing up a report. He look impossibly large hunched over the small machine, and as she had hundreds of time before, she sat across from him in the empty chair, waiting for him to finish what he was doing. Nobody else was in the office. Scott was usually the only officer on duty, and Dispatch--who also served as reception and secretary--was already gone for the day, leaving them alone.

She knew he would finish his reports, then check on any animals in the pound, taking the dogs for a walk. Then he'd seek either her or his family out for a little downtime.

"Guess what?" Amber asked, when he finally pushed himself away from his keyboard. "I have a sister!"

Shoot. So much for her promise to her mother that she'd keep her secret safe. But there was no way Amber could deal with something this huge on her own. She needed someone to talk to. She needed Scott.

"It's confidential," she added hastily.

"Okay." Scott studied her face, but remained quiet, listening.

"Not only that, but I think I may have found her. I want to wait until the government has confirmed it before I tell my mom, but my sister wants to meet. Tomorrow."

As she spilled the secret, Amber kept waiting for something to click. For it all to feel real. For the hole inside to somehow backfill, making her into some sort of elegant, mature woman who could run the PTA without accidentally giving all the fund-raising money to a charlatan. Someone Scott would be proud to have on his arm.

She was thinking of him again. Why did every thought seem to act like a Scott-magnetized boomerang these days? It went out into the world perfectly fine, but always turned midflight and landed at Scott's wonderful size eleven feet.

"I think my mom has always wondered about my sister, but she's scared to open that can of worms. I can't decide if it's better to go see this possible sister and report back to Mom, or wait. If I wait, she might say no. And if she says no then I can never go forward."

Scott stared at Amber contemplatively.

"Well?" she asked. "What do you think? What should I do?"

He folded his hands and leaned forward.

"I could use more family," she prompted, hoping he'd reply, "Go for it."

If she had his blessing, she'd know she wasn't being impulsive and that she wasn't fooling herself with false logic.

"It's exciting. The idea of having all this family out there. It's not just me and Mom. We have a *clan*."

"I know where you're coming from," Scott said at last. "But how will your mom feel if you go out and meet her while she's away? Will she feel betrayed? Is she ready to let this come out in the open? I didn't know you had a sister--this is pretty big."

"You don't know everything," Amber said, hoping the doubt she felt wasn't evident in her voice.

"I'm a cop in Blueberry Springs." He paused to let that sink in. "I know more than Mary Alice and Liz combined."

Shoot. Okay. Regroup. New argument.

There wasn't one.

"So, what should I do?"

"You can't wait, can you?"

"No." Amber practically exploded, her limbs flying out from her sides. "I'm like a cat using up all nine lives due to the depth of my curiosity on this one."

"I chased a few more reporters out of town today."

Changing the subject. She knew that tactic; she used it all the time to get out of tricky conversations.

"I should find her, shouldn't I?"

"They were snooping around, interviewing people about you. You need to watch what you do with these family secrets. These guys will be following you, digging up dirt. If they catch wind that you're trying to find your sister *and* father, they could blow up everything. I don't think that's how you want to be introduced to new family members."

"So that means I should move fast, right? Beat them to the punch?"

Scott had missed a spot shaving this morning and there was a small fuzzy patch under his chin she wanted to test with a finger, longing to know if the bristles were soft or sharp. Longing to know how they would feel against her skin.

And there she went again. The Scott boomerang. She really needed to stop or she'd end up like Liz's niece Nicola, drooling over her best friend. And that girl was drooling worse than a dog in front of a juicy steak that was tantalizingly out of reach.

"What I'm saying is that this knowledge could ruin someone's life if exposed in the wrong way," Scott said.

"Being my father or sister could ruin their life?" Amber knew she was misinterpreting his words, but she couldn't help it. "Nice. Like the past two weeks haven't been bad enough, Scott. Thanks for that."

She stood, heading for the door, but he came up behind her and wrapped his arms around her. She leaned away from his embrace, not ready to be coddled into forgiveness.

"Stop and think about it," he whispered.

"Wouldn't someone want to know if he had a daughter? Even if it was me?"

Scott turned her around, brushing a tear from her cheek, still holding her close.

"Oh, Amber." He gave her a sweet smile so full of what looked like it could be love that she wanted to will more tears onto her cheeks so he could brush them away. So he could allow her to be vulnerable and take some of the pressure from her life.

"You have to look outside yourself," he said. "Maybe your father has another family who wouldn't take too kindly to the fact that he has a child he's never acknowledged. Ignoring your family is not something to be proud of. It's not an easy thing to face."

"Mom said she didn't tell him about me."

"Then maybe she kept it a secret for a very good reason. And sometimes the longer you wait, the worse it feels when it comes to demolishing secrets."

"People need to focus less on themselves and what others think of them," Amber said, her voice muffled by the cave of his arms.

Scott chuckled. "I agree. And I also have a plan that will help satisfy your curiosity, as well as respect your mother's privacy. Ready to hear it?"

She tipped her head up to look at him, touching the spot of fuzz under his chin. It was soft but sharp-edged at the same time.

"Ready as ever."

AMBER STOOD outside the gated community in the nearby city Dakota, pacing. Scott had driven her to the neighborhood after she'd given him the info she'd compiled on Delia. They planned to do a drive-by, but nothing too stalkerish. Just a little something to help quench her curiosity and make her less antsy while she waited for her mother to return home.

Scott rubbed his chin and stared at the gate, his mouth opening as though he was about to say something. His window was down and Amber could tell he was considering all the possible ways of entering the closed community.

Should they hit the buzzer for her half sister's house and tell the truth about why they were there? Pretend to deliver pizza? Maybe just hit all the buttons in hope that someone would let them in, no questions asked? Jump the gate?

"Are you going to ram it?" Amber asked hopefully, when Scott finally looked away from the buzzer, his grip tightening on his truck's steering wheel.

He gave her an amused glance. "Is that really how you want to introduce yourself to the woman who may be your half sister? And I just had this baby repainted." He patted the side of his classic Ford truck.

Amber glanced at the thick gates again, fingers of dread clenching her stomach. She had dreams of her and her sister being similar. Of seeing herself reflected through familiar but different eyes. That she would somehow see in her sibling that piece she was missing inside herself. But now, looking at the posh gated community, Amber started to believe that maybe she was missing the half her sister possessed and it could never be found and patched in. Half of her sister came from someone else's genes. The half that made her a success.

Her sibling lived in a community with its own lake and a gate. Not a three-inch-high plastic fence propped around some wilted petunias and a mud puddle.

A vehicle drove in, the gate opening.

"Shall we?" Scott asked, putting his truck in gear. He rested his foot on the brake, waiting for Amber to give him the go-ahead.

Through the open window she placed a hand on his forearm, holding him back. The gate began to close and she quickly whacked his arm, encouraging him to speed through before it shut. Scott complied and Amber jogged alongside, the black metal gates sealing behind them. He stopped on the other side and she hopped into the passenger seat.

"Whew," she said. "That was close."

"You're nuts."

"You're the one who went for it."

"You told me to."

"I didn't say a word."

"Remember," Scott warned, "no ambushing. We're simply doing a curiosity-fueled drive-by."

"Right. No being the creepy person who tracked her down."

"It might be a little too late for that," he muttered as he turned onto a wide boulevard lined with large homes, manicured lawns and gardens surprisingly lush for the earliness of the season. The evening sun gave everything a haze that made it seem idyllic and unreal. Amber hadn't even realized there were homes like this in Dakota. As they drove by one with a pool house and guest cottage, she tried not to daydream about what it might be like if she and her sister got along famously. Would she move into their guesthouse and join her sister for coffee every morning before work?

Then the doubt began.

"What if we don't have anything in common?"

Scott, his arm resting on the frame of the open window glanced at her. "You have the same mom."

"But we obviously lead entirely different lives. I doubt she's ever dropped an ex-boyfriend's trailer off a cliff."

"You get along with everyone, Amber. It will be fine."

Scott slammed on the brakes, narrowly missing an old dog. The golden retriever meandered down the middle of the pavement, blocking their way, sparing them a glance. They were still two houses from her sister's, and Amber didn't want to stop. She wanted to keep going, hurry along, not be noticed. At the same time she wanted to ask Scott to find an excuse for her to stop and gawk, absorb every detail about the area and her possible-sister's home.

"Thank you for stopping," a woman called with a wave, and Amber slumped down in her seat. The woman left the sidewalk and called to the dog, which ignored her, continuing on his way.

"Sorry! He's deaf and old." She wore capris that fit amazingly, and Amber looked down at her own worn jeans. Maybe she should have dressed up more so she wouldn't look so out of place. No, it didn't matter. She wasn't meeting anyone and definitely not her sister. They were just passing through. Nobody would notice her.

The dog lay down in the middle of the street, blocking their way, oblivious to the truck wanting by. The young woman gave a frustrated shrug and tried to tug at his large shoulders, but he didn't budge, seeming to have decided this was a good place for a rest.

Scott pulled the vehicle to the curb and parked.

"What are you doing? We're practically in front of my sister's house," Amber whispered. "What if she looks out her window and realizes it's me?"

"And how is she going to recognize you? Does stalking run in the family?" He shut off the engine and opened his door.

"But what if she sees me today and then when we meet she remembers me and realizes I was hanging around her house and being creepy?"

"Then hide in the backseat. I don't care. But we're getting nowhere with Old Yeller in the middle of the road. They need help."

Scott walked over to the dog, which turned his head but remained where he was. Scott chatted with the woman before talking to the retriever, scratching his belly, then eventually trying to lift him. The dog growled and Scott backed off.

Amber sighed and got out of the truck. They needed to move before things got out of hand or embarrassing. She bent low and slapped her thighs, using a high-pitched, excited voice to call the dog. The animal turned his head and she encouraged him, continuing to coo. "Thatta boy! Come here. That's a good doggy." The retriever stood, joints stiff, tail moving. He waggled over to her before sitting on her feet and looking up at her with a happy smile. She petted him and gave Scott a smug look.

"Thank you so much," said the woman. "He's gotten so old he just does whatever he wants."

"You don't always have to be old to do that," Scott said under his breath, giving Amber a glance.

She replied to his comment by sticking out her tongue. He grinned. Always so darn cute.

"He usually doesn't like anyone but me." The woman gave her a long look as Amber continued to pet the dog, bracing herself as he leaned more weight against her legs. The woman's gaze came to rest on Amber's hands, and she tried to hide them in the retriever's shaggy fur. She probably had dirt under her chewed nails, from trying to get the little plastic fence around her flowers to stay upright. She doubted anyone touched dirt or chewed their nails in this part of town.

"She's great with dogs," Scott said.

"Thankfully." The woman studied Amber, apparently unable to look away from someone so obviously out of place. "I'm Delia." She reached out to shake hands, and Amber froze.

Delia?

How many Delias lived in any given neighborhood?

Amber weakly shook the woman's hand, barely daring to breathe. A young couple walked by with a baby stroller, and Delia turned to say hello to them. Amber backed away, giving them room to pass, trying to get Scott to flee with her.

"Oh, where are my manners?" Delia laughed, drawing Scott and Amber back in. "These are my neighbors, the Lunts. They're over from the UK with their beautiful baby girl, Blossom. Isn't she adorable?" Delia commandeered the stroller, turning it to face Amber and Scott. "Every time I see that darling little face it makes my own biological clock start ticking a little louder."

Amber smiled at the baby, who rewarded her with a gummy grin. Amber laughed. "She is pretty adorable."

"I babysit her whenever I can steal her away."

The parents laughed, then leaned in to share a quick peck, making Amber wish she could have something like that.

Someday.

She was going to figure out this Thompson bad-luck gene and break it. Defeat it. Overcome it. And her sister was going to help her.

"I'm Scott," he said, shaking everyone's hand, and Amber reminded herself to bury the man's body somewhere nobody would think to look. The last thing she needed was introductions that would undoubtedly lead Delia to figure out there was a connection between this Amber and the one she had been emailing.

"They helped me with Sasquatch," Delia said, tugging her dog closer. "This is…" She held out her hand to Amber. "I'm sorry, I didn't catch your name."

"Amber," she said, while clearing her throat.

"Sorry? Amber?"

She nodded reluctantly.

"You know it's funny, I met an Amber just the other day," Delia said thoughtfully. "It's not a common name."

"Neither is Delia," she said, staring at the cracks in the sidewalk. Fancy places shouldn't have cracks, but this one did. The idea was strangely comforting.

The Lunts said goodbye and continued their walk.

"Well, we should go," Amber said quickly.

"Right. Good luck with your dog," Scott stated.

"You look familiar," Delia said, stopping Amber.

"Oh, just a common face."

"No, I saw you on the news! That's where. What was it? You're an author or something?"

"I get that a lot. Nice to meet you." Amber began hurrying to the truck, but found the dog following her, blocking her way with his body, allowing his owner to catch up.

Scott opened the door for Amber, and Delia, as if sensing she was about to lose them, blurted out, "But it's something else, beyond the book. You're familiar, like I've met you before."

"Yeah, weird, right?" Amber was feeling the same way and it made her uncomfortable, only she knew why.

She gave Scott a look. It was supposed to be a drive-by. This was definitely more than that and it was all his fault.

"Do you have a sister?" Delia asked.

Amber froze and she could feel Scott watching, waiting for hints on how to proceed.

"She does," he said finally, turning to face the woman. "A half sister. Named Delia."

"Oh. My. Word." Delia elbowed Scott out of the way and threw herself on Amber, giving her a massive hug that made her spine pop. "You're Amber Thompson! I just knew it. You came and found me."

"Delia Whitehart?" Amber said meekly into the woman's glossy hair. Her cloud of expensive perfume was enveloping Amber in a way that made her feel a bit like Dorothy must have when entering Oz.

"I've wanted to meet you so badly since our emails. Waiting to see if the government gives us a confirmed match is *killing* me. Look at Sass--Sasquatch. I think he knew who you were. He won't leave your side." She held her hand out beside Amber's. "We have the same hands." Her eyes became dewy. "I've never looked like anyone in my family. This is such a strange feeling. I can't believe you found me."

Amber gave a sheepish smile. "Yeah, um, surprise?"

<hr>

As Amber allowed her possible-sister to lead her down the street and into the largest entry she'd ever seen on a single family home, she tried to talk herself down. Delia might not actually be her sibling. They had the same hands and the dates lined up, but it didn't mean they were sisters for real.

There was still a possibility it was nothing more than coincidence.

But what were the chances? They *had* to be sisters.

All Amber's visions of her and Delia being best buds flew out the window as her sister--her slim sister, who obviously had better genes--began talking about the success of her husband, and the many trips they took. She had perfect everything and the confidence to go with it.

Amber felt immensely out of place.

"Try some of this tea," Delia said, settling Amber in at her kitchen counter. "It's grown at an altitude that gives it more caffeine. It gives you an awesome kick."

"Really?" Amber peered into her cup. So far, Scott had remained quiet, sitting beside her on a stool while Delia used a ridiculous amount of gadgets before handing Amber what was essentially a mug of hot water with tea leaves drifting to the bottom.

"I have no clue. That's what the salesperson said."

Scott chuckled.

Delia watched expectantly as Amber took a tentative sip of the steaming liquid. "What do you think?"

Amber lowered the cup and gave a noncommittal nod. "Mmm. I like it." It was actually pretty decent, although she wasn't sure about a kick. "Have you tried walnut green tea?"

"It's my favorite."

"Mine, too. Do you like peanut butter on Ritz crackers?"

Her sister opened a cupboard door and waved at several boxes of the crackers in question. "I do."

"That's really specific," Scott said.

"This is so incredible." Delia sat across from Amber, shaking her head in wonder. "So amazing. It just blows your mind and makes it stop working, doesn't it?"

"Yeah, kinda," Amber said, sipping her tea. She didn't know what to think, how to react. She wanted to know everything, but at the same time needed some room to process it all. Her sister. She had a sister. And they had stunning similarities despite their vast differences.

They had to be related. If they weren't, the universe had a twisted sense of humor.

"Scott," Delia asked, "what about you? What do you do?"

"I'm a police officer."

"Such a tough job."

"It has its moments. Blueberry Springs is pretty good, though."

"He's very good at it," Amber said, resting a hand temporarily over Scott's. "Really. And he runs an animal shelter, too. Every spring and fall he always finds good homes for all the unwanted kittens."

Scott's cheeks became tinged with pink.

"Do you have any kids?" Amber asked her sister. She had a feeling she didn't, but still hoped there were little nieces and nephews she could spoil. She'd always assumed it was a privilege she'd never have.

"No, but we're thinking about it."

"How long have you and your husband been together?"

"Darren and I have been sweethearts since high school. We dated all through college over in Oxford--I love England--then we came home, got married and started our own business."

"Wow." Someone had definitely hogged the family's lucky-in-love good juju.

"How long have you two been together?" Delia asked, flicking a shiny nail between Amber and Scott.

"Oh, we're just friends." The heat that poured into Amber's face was probably telling Delia stories she didn't want revealed. Assuming there were stories. Which there weren't. They were friends. Friends who kind of had inappropriate thoughts about each other. Or at least she did. Increasingly often.

"Sorry. You must be very close friends. You're obviously very comfortable around each other."

"Best friends since the day I moved to town as a kid." Scott gave Amber an affectionate ear tug. "Amber stayed in at recess and made me a valentine so I'd have one."

"He moved on Valentine's Day," Amber added.

"That's sweet," her sister said. "Blueberry Springs sounds incredible."

"It is pretty nice," Amber agreed. "I'm hoping to move back to the city soon, but the town's pretty good. It's where I grew up, and there are festivals and fairs. Stuff like that. And the people look out for each other and make it feel like home, I guess. You know small towns."

"Why would you move back to the city?" Delia asked. "The place sounds sweet."

"Well, I just think…" Amber paused. How could she explain to her sister that she felt as though there were more opportunities to be someone other than she was, without making it sound as if she was ungrateful for all their mother had done?

"Why *do* you want to move back?" Scott asked quietly.

"Uh, jobs?"

"You don't like yours any longer?"

"What do you do?" Delia asked.

"Database management. And the job is fine. I can do it anywhere. I just like the fact that nobody is in my business in the city, I guess. There's freedom to reinvent yourself frequently."

Not that she was eager to reinvent herself again, seeing as last time she'd ended up in a book. Sometimes it was just easier to be herself. Which was the nice thing about Blueberry Springs. She had the same old routines. Everyone knew her and could predict when she'd want a slice of pie, and she didn't have to explain anything to anyone back home. They already knew, and there was surprising comfort in that.

Plus the people in Blueberry Springs really weren't so bad. They meant well and had been pretty supportive about the book. Mary Alice had even stopped selling it in her store once she realized how much it bothered Amber.

She'd moved to the city in hopes of becoming someone "big." And she had. Although making it "big" in Russell's book hadn't been great so far. She'd prefer to feel important, valued, and as though she made a difference. She wanted to be someone people counted on, wanted, and needed. Someone who would be missed.

She hadn't had that in the city. In fact, none of her friends there had contacted her after the book had come out other than to send a few texts asking if she wanted to come to a party. Amber had seen them for what they were--not asking if she was okay or how she was doing, simply wanting to leech her semi-fame. Well, they could have it. She wanted to be more than a pawn, where once her service was over she'd get knocked off the game board and they'd all continue on without her.

"We should probably go," Scott said, standing. "Thank you for the tea. It was a pleasure meeting you."

"What's our mom like?" Delia asked, stepping forward, her eyes so full of unexpected need that Amber leaned into Scott, looking at him to guide her through this.

"She's..." She couldn't say a "great mom," because what if that made Delia feel as though she'd lost out? Amber didn't want to say "waitress" and have Delia judge her for that. "You'll have to meet her. She's nice."

"I would love that so much. Can I meet her soon? Does she know we're emailing? I'm free tomorrow. I know that's sudden, but after all this time waiting and hoping, it's just so hard to wait any longer."

"I know, but, well, it's... complicated."

As they drove out of the gated community, Amber let out a sigh of relief. "I didn't screw that up too badly, did I?"

"You were great."

"Thanks for coming with me." There was nobody she'd rather have with her. Amber reached over and squeezed Scott's hand, a fissure of electricity rolling up her arm at their touch.

"Do you think she's your sister?"

"Yes. Although she was nothing like what I expected."

"What did you expect?"

"I don't know. Me, but different."

"I think she is you, but different. You both light up in the same way when you're excited."

Amber cut him a glance. What did that mean? And why did she feel jealous? Was this sibling rivalry? If so, that was mighty quick and she wasn't sure if she liked it. In fact, she knew she didn't.

"Milkshake?" Scott asked, pulling into their favorite drive-through burger joint in Dakota.

"Yeah." Her stomach rumbled. She'd missed supper with their excursion. "And a cheeseburger."

"Two large chocolate milkshakes and two cheeseburgers," Scott said into the microphone.

"She has everything."

"Who? Delia?"

Amber nodded.

Scott scooted off his butt so he could dig his wallet from his back pocket. His thighs were tensed as he twisted, his hips so narrow, yet powerful. She focused on the line of cars in front of them so she wouldn't get caught checking him out, or the bulge… wow. Yep. She needed to get her brain checked. Her eyes were drifting to zones that were marked Lovers Only.

"I didn't realize you were looking for a senile dog and a husband who works away a lot," Scott said, letting out a chuckle.

"Ha ha. But look at her. She's gorgeous. Skinny. Amazing house. Successful life. She's confident. Perfect."

"Not being perfect is what makes *you* so darn likable." Scott gave her a smile so warm it made her stomach feel funny. In a good way.

"When it comes right down to it, Officer Malone, you're not that far off a truckload of 'not bad' yourself."

As they waited for their milkshakes Amber wondered if her sister represented the life she herself could have if she managed to pull it together, started believing in herself and stopped making stupid man choices.

She said, "When I saw her neighborhood I thought she couldn't be anything like me and that we'd hate each other. But I could kind of see hanging out with her. Even though she kicks my butt in terms of pretty much everything other than having excellent hips for hip checking."

"Ah, the trash-yourself segment of today's show. Why do you do that?" Scott turned in his seat, gripping her headrest as he took her in. It almost felt as though he was prepping to lean in and kiss her, but she knew better. He knew she didn't think of him in that way. Still, she couldn't help but notice that he smelled wonderful and that his chin had a slight five o'clock shadow that would feel sharp, yet pleasing against her skin.

"She kind of brought out some of my insecurities." Amber rubbed her thighs with the heels of her hands.

"You were great with her dog. You were kind and sensitive when dealing with her, too. Thoughtful and considerate. There's nothing to berate yourself over."

"Do you think she'll like me?"

"It sounded as though she wants to see you again, so yes. And who couldn't love Amber Thompson, anyway?"

She almost asked, "Do you?" Instead, she said, "What should I do about my mom?"

"Tell her the truth."

"But…"

They were handed their milkshakes and burgers. Scott drove toward the edge of the city, where they would take the highway to Blueberry Springs.

"But what?" he finally asked.

"How do I explain doing all of this stuff behind her back?"

"Just tell her."

They passed a police station near the edge of the city and Amber wondered if it would be the one Scott would be working out of when he transferred. When he left. He hadn't said anything about an interview. Hadn't said anything about applying, either.

"I really screwed up, didn't I?" she said, unwrapping her burger. She was losing so much, so quickly. It was as if she was finding the things she loved best just in time to lose them.

"Be careful," Scott advised, taking a sip of his milkshake. "Don't give Delia too much personal information. She's still a stranger even though we believe she's your sister."

"Yeah. Might be too late for that." Her sister knew where she lived and Amber had opened the door for "pop on by" with her accidental visit today.

Scott's brow furrowed as he stopped in a line of traffic waiting at a road construction site. He twisted in his seat again, facing her, her body half cocooned by him with his arm across her seat back. Outside, the sun was setting, the spring air giving the green foothills a glow.

"Do you think there's a chance she'll come by to check out the town before your mom returns?"

"She is my sister."

Scott was openly admiring her and Amber wondered what it would be like to allow herself the opportunity to change things between them. What would happen if she gave in to her restless thoughts about him?

She slowly leaned across the console that separated them, watching him carefully. He looked curious, but not at all as if expecting her to graze his lips with hers. She kissed him, almost drawing away before he began reciprocating, his mouth cool and sweet from the milkshake. Heat flooded through Amber, touching areas she hadn't even known existed. Still kissing, she placed her hands on either side of his mouth, wishing she could climb into his lap and continue this forever.

Just when she thought she'd become lost in him, he broke the kiss, leaning away.

"I thought you wanted this," she said, trying to ignore the slice of rejection that had cut her open.

Scott was silent for a moment before gently cupping her cheek, caressing it with a rough thumb. "Amber," he said softly, "you will always be worth waiting for."

"There's no wait. I'm right here." She swallowed hard, uncertain as to why she was crossing the line she had so vigilantly avoided for years, and even more uncertain as to why he was pushing her away. "I'm ready. Ready for this. For us." Her voice was shaking from the fear ripping through her chest.

"You're not."

"I am." Her voice became soft, her tone begging.

"You're not ready, Amber, and both you and I know it."

She stuck out her chin. "I'm ready, Officer Malone."

He swallowed, his gaze darkening with something she couldn't identify, but she knew it wasn't anger. He wanted her, and yet he was saying no.

"I'm not good enough?" She would never be a mayor or a beauty queen or any of the amazing women Scott had dated. But she'd always secretly hoped, way back in the furthest reaches of her mind, that she would be enough for him. She'd been wrong.

"Amber, don't go down that road." His eyes were like fire. "You know you're not ready. I can see it in your eyes."

"No. I want you."

"You don't." His voice was harsh.

She did. She wanted him. Her best friend. She wanted to fall into his strength and shelter. And that kiss... it had been the beginning of something. Something she'd never felt before. How could he not see that?

"This is too important to mess up," he said. "When you're ready we'll start something good."

"No."

"No?" He quirked a brow, leaning on the console, practically daring her to argue.

"I'm ready and I demand you be my boyfriend. Now." She pointed at the floorboards of the truck.

Scott's lips turned up.

"And you love me?" he asked, his tone half teasing, half full of some sort of magical heat that turned her mind to mush. The pads of his fingers grazed the back of her neck, sending shivers through her core.

Amber tried to form words. *Love.* She loved the way he was touching her. His voice. The way he made her feel when he was around.

"As a friend?" he offered. She nodded, before catching herself and shaking her head. No. That wasn't right, was it? That wasn't what he was looking for.

Her heart felt dizzy and her mind had lost its bearings. What did she want? What did she feel? She loved him as more than a friend. She had to. How could she not, after a kiss like that?

He took one glance back at her before steering the truck into the now-flowing traffic, his jaw set with determination. "When you're truly ready, Amber Lynn Thompson. But I won't take you a moment before."

6

Waitressing was the most difficult job Amber had ever had. It didn't help that the only thing she could concentrate on was Scott, their kiss, and the way he'd told her she wasn't ready. Of course she was ready. He hadn't even given her a chance to say she loved him.

The customers at Benny's were demanding and impatient. They wanted to chat her ear off, while having her magically bring them their meals at the same time. If she wanted a tip--and she did--she had to stand there with a smile and listen to them discuss how alike she and her mother were. That and the book. When were she and Scott going to get together, anyway?

If one more person asked that, Amber was going to cry. She'd tried. She'd been rejected. And every time someone mentioned the subject it felt as though the knife was being driven in a little deeper.

The lunch rush finally ended and the restaurant quieted down to the point where she could sit for a minute to eat her own lunch. Amber had no idea how her mother did this all day. Every day for decades.

Benny came over with a cup of coffee and sat across from her. "Looks like you'll make out okay for tips."

"Because they feel sorry for me and I'm Gloria's daughter."

"You did well, though. Not many errors. A natural, like your mom."

"Yeah, like my mom." Amber squelched the volcanic eruption inside her that fought against the idea, and picked at her salad before finally pushing it away.

"It'll start getting busy around three for the coffee break, and then again around five-thirty for supper. You know what it's like. You've spent almost as much time in here as your mom. When you're done lunch, I'll show you a few things you can do ahead of time to make it easier when the next rush hits."

"Thanks." Amber tried to smile and look grateful for the help. She'd seen her mother do pre-rush prep and had a pretty good idea what needed to be done, but didn't want to screw things up or make it harder than it already was.

A while later, Mary Alice and Liz came in for an early supper. Since the dawn of time the two had met up at Benny's every week to chat and laugh. Amber couldn't help but wonder if one day she and Delia would have weekly or monthly get-togethers, too. She kind of hoped so. It would be nice to have a sibling to lean on and build a history with. And Delia seemed so together that she'd be an ultimate big sister. She'd barely been fazed at finding her sister on her neighborhood street, and had assumed the best, not that Amber was creepy--thankfully.

"Amber, hon." Mary Alice waved her over. "We're ready to settle up." She dipped a hand down the neck of her blouse and rummaged through her bra, finally pulling out a tin of mints as well as a small change purse that contained a few bills.

Amber passed them their check, pleased to have remembered to give them a discount for the daily special.

"You are so much like your mother," Mary Alice said, reaching up to pat Amber's cheek. "Although Gloria doesn't need a notepad to remember our orders." She gave Amber a playful look.

"It's her first day," Liz said, coming to Amber's defense. "Plus you always order the same thing and have for the past fifteen years."

"Say…" began Mary Alice, changing the subject. Amber figured she was warming up to start running interference in someone's life or else divulge the latest gossip. It was amazing how many people had told her things "confidentially" today. Being a waitress was similar to being a storehouse for secrets. No wonder her mother felt so at home with the job.

"Nicola--our niece--needs a distraction," Mary Alice finished.

Amber sure could use one, too. She couldn't stop thinking about Scott and the way his quads had flexed under the cover of his jeans as he'd driven them home last night. The way his shoulders rounded when he was fed up with her. How he'd said no.

How would she ever show him she was ready?

Maybe *he* wasn't ready.

Now there was a thought.

Amber quirked her head, struggling to stay focused on her customers. "I thought Nicola was busy with her community planning job."

"She's almost done her part on that new subdivision. We never see her because of the long hours, but now she's wrapping it up."

Liz jumped in. "And so Nicola's going to need a new distraction."

"Did someone say Nicola Samuels needs a distraction?" Devon Mattson, Mandy's oldest brother, asked as he joined the ladies at their table, helping himself to Liz's mostly untouched fries. He gave Amber a large grin, illustrating that he knew just how handsome and supposedly irresistible he was. "I'm available for distracting women."

"You always are," Amber said. "Is it any wonder?" The man was a daredevil playboy.

"Don't feel left out. There's plenty of me to go around." He winked at her.

"You stay away from our niece," Mary Alice scolded. "She doesn't need your kind of wildness."

"What about me? You're not going to protect me from this big lump?" Amber asked, smacking Devon's chest. She blinked away images of Scott coming and rescuing her from Devon's clutches.

My goodness. She needed to get over whatever it was that was messing with her mind. Such as that kiss. Man, that had been good.

"I'm not wild," Devon replied, arms out as though that proved his innocence.

"Right," Liz said with an eye roll. "And I wear shorts in snowstorms."

"I'm sure it's happened. Zip out to grab the newspaper off the front step while wearing your husband's oversize shirt and boxers?" he teased.

He was rewarded by a glare.

Mary Alice continued, "What do you think we could distract her with?" She pointed a finger at Devon. "Don't say it."

"Summer is coming," Amber offered. "She used to travel and hike and stuff, didn't she? When she went around the world with Todd? Maybe she could help Jen."

"Aha!" Devon slapped the table in triumph. "This is about Todd, isn't it? You want him to get her, not me."

The sisters ignored him.

"Jen's wilderness guiding business is expanding."

"And she's pregnant?" Mary Alice added, looking hopefully at anyone who would offer confirmation.

The group let out a collective sigh, and Amber said, "But I don't quite get what she needs the distraction from." She pointed to Devon and mouthed, "*Him?*"

Mary Alice shook her head.

"I do like that idea--helping Jen," Liz said, tapping her chin thoughtfully.

"Are we really just trying to distract her from Devon?" Amber asked, as though the man in question wasn't sitting at the table, listening intently.

"Todd," the sisters said simply.

Devon and Amber shared a look.

"What do you mean?" Amber asked. She had thought the two friends were going to get together at the Valentine's Day extravaganza, but assumed they hadn't, since she hadn't seen Todd around. Since then, Nicola had all but disappeared into her job, losing weight in the process. Amber hadn't thought much of it, but now she wondered. Nicola used to barely be able to take a breath without talking about her BFF Todd, yet Amber could barely recall the last time he or their grand travel adventures had been mentioned. What had happened? And how had Amber managed to push her head so far up her own butt that she hadn't even noticed the changes in her friend?

"What's going on out there?" Liz asked, craning her neck to look through the big windows that faced the sidewalk. "Don't tell me there are more reporters in town." She stood, straightening her floral blouse. "Oh, well. I chased them out of Blueberry Springs when they were harassing Jen. The least I can do is chase them out for you, too." She smiled at Amber and hustled to the door.

Amber followed, not quite sure whether Liz would make things better or not.

On the sidewalk, Amber blinked and looked again. She did *not* just see who she thought she had. Nope. Sure enough, there was a television van, but that's not what had caught her eye. It was her sister. Talking to a reporter.

What was she doing in town? And why was she talking to the media? This could not be good.

A cluster of onlookers had gathered, their ears tilted toward Delia as though they were afraid they would miss something. Collectively, they all leaned back in apparent awe, before glancing at each other and leaning in again.

No way that could be a positive. Her mother's secret was going to be revealed to the entire world because Amber had a problem with being impulsive. And so, too, might Delia.

Amber tried to control her anger as she walked toward her sister and the reporter, waving Liz, Mary Alice, and Devon back.

"I'm not local," Delia was saying. "No, I don't have an opinion about the town or Amber Thompson or Russell Peaks. I'm here to try the brownies at the Wrap It Up, as I've heard they're to die for." She glanced at Amber and they shared a look.

"You know Amber?" the reporter asked, noticing the exchange.

"I do," Delia said carefully.

"In what capacity?" He was eyeing Amber in a way she wasn't comfortable with.

"We met the other day. She's a lovely, helpful woman. That will be all. Thank you." She shook the reporter's hand, doing an excellent job of removing herself from the interview.

Amber could have hugged her, her relief was so intense. Her sister was her hero. She'd just disarmed a reporter.

As Amber went to join her, wondering how to approach her arrival, she could have sworn she heard someone in the crowd say "related."

Liz drew Amber to the side before she got to Delia. "Who is she? She seems familiar somehow."

"Delia Whitehart," Amber said, with no further explanation. She reached her sister, snagging her by the arm and pivoting them back toward Benny's restaurant, seeing as she was still on shift.

"Thank you," Amber whispered as she held the door open for

her, noting that the reporter was now badgering Blueberry Springs residents, who were frowning at her, arms crossed.

"I hope I didn't say anything that could complicate things for you. I had no idea. I was dropping off paperwork in Derbyshire and thought I'd drive through to take a peek at the town."

"What I heard was perfect. You're a lifesaver." Amber settled her sister at a table. "I'm helping out here," she said, catching herself before she said she was covering for their mother. Too much personal information, and info she wasn't at liberty to give out, even though she felt Delia had the right to know. "I'm not off for a few more hours, but if you'd like a slice of pie or something I could get you one on the house. Benny, the owner, won't mind."

"Are you sure? I wouldn't want to get you in trouble."

"I'm sure it will be fine. Chocolate okay?"

"Silly question. Of course chocolate. Hit me up!"

Amber went to the kitchen for a slice of pie, automatically including a glass of milk.

"I'm lactose intolerant," Delia said, frowning at the milk. "Sorry."

"No, I should have asked." Amber picked up the glass again, holding it awkwardly. "Um, the pie has cream in it."

"Don't worry." She fished some pills out of her purse. "These will handle the pie. A glass of milk is just a bit more than they can cover."

"Delia?" Amber perched on the edge of the chair across from her. "Did you know you were going to marry your husband the first time you met him?"

"Nah, I decked him the day we met. He kissed me right there on the playground." Her sister smiled, her cheeks pinking at the memory. That woman loved her man something fierce. "We had to spend recess indoors, but by the end of our punishment we were friends. He didn't try to kiss me again until we were thirteen."

"Scott and I have been best friends since forever." Amber pressed her fingers to her lips as she thought of their kiss.

Delia nodded encouragingly and Amber hesitated before deciding that what she could use right now was some romance advice from a big sister. Her lucky-in-love big sister.

"I kissed him when we were coming home from the city. I thought he wanted more. Everyone keeps saying he loves me and has since forever." She paused, feeling embarrassed for outing Scott's feelings to a woman who was still essentially a stranger. "And sometimes the look in his eyes…" Amber felt the sting of his rejection once again. "He said no."

"No?"

"He doesn't think I'm ready."

"And are you?"

Amber nodded, despite the uncertainty eroding her confidence. Was this what Scott was talking about? But she couldn't imagine her life without him. That had to mean she was ready. So why couldn't she tell the most important man in her life that she loved him? She knew she did, and she'd said those three small words to past boyfriends without issue, so it wasn't as though she had troubles forming the words. But whenever she thought of telling Scott, she felt as though a huge weight settled on her vocal cords. It was as though once those three tiny words were said she would never be able to take them back and her whole world would become entirely different. It would change everything.

"Thanks again for sorting out my ordering system, Amber," Benny called, drawing Amber from her thoughts. He paused as he walked by with his daily deposit for the bank.

Amber waved at him absently. Maybe she *wasn't* ready for Scott. But what would she need to do in order to be ready?

"Well, now," Benny continued. "You two could pass for sisters. What? Why are you looking at me like that?"

The sisters shared a glance.

"Oh." Benny nodded and kept going. "Okay." He paused with his hand on the door, then muttered something to himself and kept going.

Amber sighed. Things were about to get complicated again.

AMBER NEEDED TO WOO SCOTT. Delia had said her husband showed his love in different ways and that words weren't everything. Maybe Amber could show Scott she cared with gestures. All she needed was a good dress and some courage. She hadn't seen him since the kiss, but she hoped that if she appeared looking amazing he would see how silly he had been to say they needed to wait.

She'd fortified herself with chocolate and coffee, worked through most of the night to get ahead on her database job, served her shift at Benny's--where she'd told her boss not to talk to a soul about Delia and that she'd tell him everything when she could--grabbed her three friends, and was ready to find The Dress. As for the courage part of the plan, Amber hoped it would appear by magic when she needed it most.

"Why do you need a dress?" Jen asked. She'd just come out of the woods after an all-day hike with clients and was wearing a T-shirt she'd designed with a hiker running from a bear, plus wrinkle-free shorts, and hiking boots. Not exactly someone who might grasp the need for the perfect dress, but Amber had chosen her for her common sense, hoping it would level out Mandy's intricate sense of style sense, given that Amber still needed to look like herself. She'd brought Nicola along to break any tie votes between the friends, and because she looked as though she could use some good old-fashioned retail therapy.

"I want to feel feminine," Amber replied.

They were in Wanda's wedding store and Amber was hoping

to find a little black dress. Or a cute red one. Or really, anything that would show her man she was ready.

"No wedding to go to?" Jen asked, eliciting a frustrated sigh from Mandy.

"She's trying to get Scott's attention," Mandy explained.

"Shh!" Amber said, casting a quick look around the store. She didn't want word getting back to Scott before she had a chance to make her move.

Mandy ignored her. "Remember? Like we did for you and Rob? The dress that made you look like Marilyn Monroe."

Jen brightened. "Oh yeah! That almost even worked." She yawned again, slumping in her seat. "But not really."

Nicola held out a dress. "I think I'm going to try this one on."

"We're here for Amber, not ourselves." Mandy reached for a dress, checked the tag, then put it back. "If I'd known you wanted to wow Scott, I could have watched for something in the designer sales I go to. Huge savings."

"Would they have my size?" Amber asked doubtfully. She didn't think designers were used to covering this much ground.

"Hi, ladies," Wanda said, joining them. "What are we looking for today? Are you planning your wedding, Mandy?" She eyed Mandy's engagement band. "Have you chosen your special date?"

"Oh." Mandy looked around the store, eyes wide. "Um. No, not yet."

"We're here for Amber," Jen said, yawning. "She wants to look 'feminine.'" She used air quotes around the word.

"Ah, want to catch a certain officer's eye, do we?" Wanda smiled knowingly and began rifling through the racks with an expert's speed.

"Um…" Amber gave her friends a feeble shrug. "Maybe?"

"Any color or style preferences?" Wanda asked, holding out three casual, summery dresses.

"Not yet," Amber said. The store was overwhelming. So many

dresses, from casually simple to wedding gowns that looked as though they should be worn by princesses.

"Who was that woman in town the other day?" Wanda asked as she handed Amber a few choices. "The one who looked like she could be your sister?"

"Delia. Are these my size?" Amber glanced at the tags. They were. Wanda was a magician.

"Any relation?" Wanda asked. She held another dress under Amber's chin before placing it back on the rack.

Amber could feel her friends watching her, wondering who Delia was, but being too polite to ask. So far.

"She does look a lot like me, doesn't she? Uncanny," she said, struggling to refrain from blurting out the exciting truth. "I'm going to try these on." Amber waved the dresses and hightailed it to the fitting room before her valve broke and her mother's secrets leaked out.

In the fitting room she took several deep breaths, relieved she hadn't said anything, but worried that she'd somehow given the others something to go on.

She tried on a dress. The style was flattering, but the fabric too flowery. Looking at the chosen items she began to doubt her plan. She wasn't even sure what would catch Scott's eye. Plus she needed to be able to wear the dress down the streets of Blueberry Springs without everyone knowing she was up to something. The plan was to woo Scott to the point where he couldn't say no. To the point where he'd realize just how serious she was.

"How does it look?" Wanda asked.

Amber opened the door and did a twirl for her audience. Jen scrunched up her face, while Mandy gazed thoughtfully.

"Size and style are right, but it's not quite you," Wanda said, turning to dive back through her racks.

"Where's Nicola?" Amber asked.

"Trying on a red number."

"Ta-da!" Nicola said, popping out of the change room next to Amber's. "What do you think?" She did a twirl and curtsy.

"You look hot." Amber tried not to let her jealousy show. The dress did all the right things for her friend, somehow shaving her hips into proportion with her small waist and chest. "Between the weight you've lost and this dress, you are going to turn heads."

"I'd better lock up Devon," Mandy said. "He'll never stop drooling over you."

"Oh, your brother doesn't scare me," Nicola said, checking the dress in the mirror.

"Nicola!" Wanda clapped her hands together, staring at her. "It's perfect on you." She flung a dress at Amber and turned away. "I also have it in midnight blue. You have to try it. It will be incredible with your blond hair."

"My brother *should* scare you," Mandy said. "That man needs stitches or casts every five months due to his daredevil ways."

"He's pretty cute," Amber said. "You should set him up with someone, Mandy. That might tame him. Keep him alive a little longer, too."

Mandy laughed. "Good luck. He's going to be a bachelor forever."

A look crossed Nicola's face and Amber felt as though she'd missed something. That was the problem about being away for a few years and then having your head up your butt. She didn't know what was going on any longer, even though Nicola had lived in Blueberry Springs only since January.

Jen, still sitting, but now with her chin propped on her fist and eyes closed, looked as though she was drifting off. So much for the common sense element helping out if needed.

Mandy held up a new green dress Wanda had brought, along with the midnight-blue one for Nicola. "This is nice. Same style as that one, different fabric. Not quite so cotton candy."

"May as well try it," Amber said, casting a glance at Nicola, who was still admiring herself in the mirror. "You need to buy that," she told her, "in every color they have. It's stunning."

A few dresses later, Amber had a simple A-line dress in emerald green she figured would do the trick. As she eyed her reflection, butterflies stormed her stomach. Could she simply practice saying the words, close her eyes, and deliver them? Problem solved? Man captured?

She whispered to the mirror, "Scott Malone, I love you to bits."

"I'm so telling Scott," Nicola teased from the room next door.

"Yeah? Then I'll tell Todd you love him."

Silence.

"Nicola?"

"Yeah? What? I'm fine!" she chirped.

"Are you decent? Expect a visitor," Amber said, unlatching her side of the fitting room partition, ready to swing it open to make one big space, like brides did when trying on large dresses. "Unlatch your side." She rapped on the wall. "Nicola?"

She heard her friend open her side and the wall swung like a door.

"You okay?" Amber asked. Nicola looked pale and worried. "What happened with Todd?"

Nicola rolled her eyes and slipped her jeans on under the dress. "Nothing."

"But you love him, don't you?"

"Let's just say I crossed the line and it didn't work out the way I had envisioned."

"What do you mean?"

"I kissed him. And I haven't seen him since."

For the first time Amber worried about the validity of her plan to woo Scott.

AMBER SMOOTHED HER DRESS, fidgeted with the loose updo she'd copied from Pinterest, and tried to summon her courage to knock on Scott's door. What if what had happened to Nicola happened to her?

She'd kissed Scott, then not seen him for a few days.

What if she'd crossed the wrong line at the wrong time?

What if leaping from best friends to lovers wasn't in their cards?

She took a huge breath, willing herself not to turn away. It was time to take action and put herself out there. Nicola's sitting around moping wasn't getting her anywhere, was it?

Amber opted for a burst of rapping with her knuckles before ducking into Scott's front entry.

"Scott? Are you home?" Silly question. Of course he was. He was one of the few people in Blueberry Springs who locked their doors when not home. If it was unlocked, he was home.

"Ever heard of an invention called a doorbell?" The groggy voice came from the living room couch. Scott sat up looking adorably disheveled--if indeed a cranky man the size of a bear could be called adorable.

"Shut up. I'm taking you out for supper."

He perked up and Amber saw a flash of the old Scott. Curious, fun-loving. Not all serious and telling her what-was-what all the time.

"Where to?"

"It's a picnic." She held up the basket. She had homemade potato salad, cucumber sandwiches, brownies from Mandy's restaurant and apple cider from Brew Babies.

"That's not taking me out," he said, falling back against the cushions to finish his nap, arm slung over his eyes.

His lips, visible below his elbow, were pursed and tempting, and she stared at them, wondering what it would be like to kiss them again. Would their kisses always be amazing? Or had it simply been the element of surprise that had made their first kiss awesome?

And why was he shutting her out instead of acting as though the one thing he'd wanted for all these years was finally going to happen--them? Maybe he'd changed his mind or didn't like the way she kissed.

He hadn't even noticed the dress, and that she was making an attempt. She stood over him, determined to make him see her.

"A picnic is taking you out. It's romantic. It's sweet. You wanted me to show you I'm ready to do this thing. I'm ready."

"'Do this thing.' You *are* so romantic." He pulled down his arm to give her a wry frown and did a double take. "What are you wearing?"

"A dress."

"Why?"

"I just said..." Her voice wavered. This wasn't how it was supposed to work. He was supposed to sweep her up into his arms or something. Not be a belligerent, question-asking, I-want-romance dude. It felt as though everything was falling apart and she didn't know how to fix it.

First Russell, then trying to keep her sister a secret. Trying to find her father, who didn't even know she existed, plus tell her mother about Delia. And now Scott. It was something about Amber. She was broken and she left brokenness in her wake.

She had naively thought finding her sister would help her piece her life together and figure out what she was missing. But she was unchanged. Still the same person.

She still wasn't in the place she wanted to be in her life and she had no clue how to get there from here.

But right now she had a choice. She could fight or she could run.

"The hardest part about moving away from home was not seeing you every day."

It was the truth, a truth she'd never shared with anyone. She hadn't missed home, or even Benny's pie. It had been Scott who had made her homesick. Fifteen times a day she had to stop herself from running back to Blueberry Springs to talk to him in person.

But it was more than that. She needed a man like him in her life. Someone to give her gentle pushback when she needed it. Someone to point out where she was steering herself wrong. Someone to lean on when things got tough. Someone to laugh with, to share humor and love--her life.

She needed Scott.

"Do you love me?" she asked.

Scott stared at her for several full seconds before she couldn't take it any longer. Placing a hand on his chest, she leaned over him, kissing him. She nibbled on his bottom lip, tugging a low groan from him. His arms wrapped around her, pulling her on top of him, her body in line with his. It felt good being held tight against him. Safe. Happy.

Scott sat up suddenly and she thought he was going to move them somewhere more private. But instead, he deposited her onto the cushion beside him and dragged his hands down his face, looking as bothered as though he'd just kissed his best friend's gal.

"What?" The single word sounded insecure, and not nearly as light and carefree as she'd intended.

"I like you, Amber."

Like? The word was a final, well-placed dagger to her already staggering heart.

"But you're not ready for this. When this happens..." He faced her on the couch, his knee pressing into hers. He pointed to his chest, then hers. "It's going to be huge. Knock your socks off, never look at another man ever again kind of special. You understand?"

Okay, wow. This version of Scott was knee-weakening in a tie me to the bed and ravish me until I can't take any more kind of amazing.

She nodded in agreement, hating herself for giving in, wishing she could find a way to make this happen right now, because she had no clue how to be more ready in the way Scott wanted or expected.

He tipped her chin up so she was forced to meet his eyes.

"You don't wait for the woman of your life and then blow it by starting before she's ready to love you in the way you need her to."

The intention and intensity in his gaze overwhelmed her. Nobody had ever said anything like that to her. Not even her ex the novelist. She felt pinned to the spot by the intensity of Scott's love and emotion, his strength and determination and his willingness to wait for exactly what he wanted. On his terms.

The way he talked about who they could be was intoxicating. He really believed they could be that incredible together. The stuff of legends.

She wanted to believe it. She wanted to lean into him, test his strength and see how long before she became completely lost in him.

He took her hand. "Believe me, Amber. We're going to be worth waiting for. Once you're ready."

A feeling of dread settled low in Amber's stomach. If they were waiting for something she was supposed to do, she feared she would never figure it out, and that their time as a couple would never come.

$\mathcal{A}$mber checked the arrivals board at the airport one last time. Her mother should be at the baggage carousel by now. Had she missed her flight?

"What time was your mom supposed to arrive?" Scott asked, glancing at his watch. Amber slipped her hand into his and he gave her a look.

She was ready and he needed to see that. There was nothing left for her to do. She was proving it right here, right now.

"Amber," he said gently, removing his hand from hers.

She was already doing her best not to kiss him; what more did he want? For her to strangle all the other women she'd seen admiring his broad, muscular build? Would that be what it took for him to see that she was serious about this? About them?

Amber caught a glimpse of a couple walking and laughing, shoulders bumping as they moved toward the baggage claim. That was what she wanted. With Scott. She blinked and looked again. The man was John Abcott. With a woman who was tanned, beaming, and looked at least five years younger than her mother.

Except it *was* her mother.

Spotting Amber, Gloria broke away from John, schooling her smile as she came over for a hug.

"Did you have a good trip?" Amber asked.

"Wonderful! I need to do this more often." She tugged John over. "And look who I ran into!"

Scott and John shook hands. "Do you need a ride?" Scott asked.

"Marisa's coming for me, but thanks. Oh, and there she is." John pointed to the dark-haired girl, who was Amber's age. "Lovely to have vacationed with you, Gloria." He gave her an affectionate look.

No. There was no way. Amber glanced at Scott to see if he was picking up on anything. He was watching them, too.

"You vacationed together?" she asked her mom, who was positively moon-eyed.

"Hmm? Yes. Same cruise," she said, studying the bags going around on the convertor. "I think that one's… no, not mine."

Amber studied her mother, who was way too focused on identifying her bag.

"Something happened on the trip," Amber said.

"What?" She started, turning a shoulder as if to block her daughter. "Oh? No. Nothing."

"You're different." Amber stepped closer, as though she would be able to smell the truth on her mother's clothes and be able to identify exactly what had happened to make her so happy. There was no way she could be in love. Not with John, anyway. The two of them were as unlikely as him being Amber's father.

Although John and Gloria had dated when they were younger. Maybe the cruise had ended up being like one of those long-lost-love-reunited specials she saw on TV.

She almost laughed out loud. Talk about unrealistic.

Gloria pointed to her suitcase and Scott plucked it off the conveyer.

"Did she stay out of trouble, Scott?" her mother asked.

His mouth twisted with amusement. "Almost" was all he said as he moved ahead with the suitcase, allowing Amber and her mother to fall in behind him.

Amber seized the opportunity and blurted out, "Mom, I met someone who I think is my sister."

Her mother stopped short.

"I was looking through online databases and I contacted a few people on a whim. A woman named Delia Whitehart replied and I think she's my sister. She is quiet, thoughtful, caring, smart, patient, successful, and lives in a gated community in Dakota. I met her and we have the same hands. And a dog. No, we don't have the same dog. She has a dog. Named Sasquatch. And she has a husband and no kids, and they run their own company. She'd like to meet you and she's been to Blueberry Springs. We look alike and I think Benny might have figured it out, but I asked him not to breathe a word."

Scott rolled his eyes at Amber and sighed.

"I'm so sorry," she said to her mother, barely daring to breathe. She hadn't meant to blurt out everything all at once, but she was nervous and afraid that her mother would interrupt and kibosh the entire topic, banishing the subject of Delia forevermore if she didn't get it all out at once for her to consider.

"You've met her?" Gloria finally said.

"She's really nice."

"They named her Delia?"

Amber nodded, feeling as though she could break into tears at any moment due to the stress of anticipating her mother's ultimate reaction. This could either bring them closer or ruin everything. Amber had crossed a line, stepping out in a way she never had before.

Scott gave her shoulder a gentle squeeze and she let out the breath she'd been holding.

"Amber's applied to the government adoption agency for confirmation that Delia is indeed her half sister," he added, his voice calming, reassuring. "Meeting Delia was truly an accident. We were scoping out the scene before Amber proceeded any further with her emails, and had a run-in."

"This is…" Gloria said quietly, taking a few small steps away "…this is a lot to take in."

Amber wasn't sure if her mother was mad, indignant, relieved, or none of the above.

"She'd like to meet you, if you're ready for that," Amber said, trying to keep a leash on her mouth. "But I'll do whatever you want me to. I'll tell people she's a cousin. Tell them the truth. I can wait. Or introduce you. Never see her again. Whatever you need."

She struggled with her emotions, not ready to give up the sister she'd only just found. But if finding her sister meant losing her mother, she'd choose her mom any day of the week from now until the end of eternity.

"I would have liked to have discussed this, Amber." Her mother's voice was careful, controlled.

"I know. I'm sorry. I should have waited. I should have asked you first. I honestly didn't think this would happen. Not so fast."

"I didn't, either," Scott added helpfully.

Her mother gazed at Scott for a long moment, then sighed and nodded, her expression softening.

"Amber, my Amber." She wrapped an arm around her, looking so much older than she had only minutes ago. "How do you manage?"

Amber bit her bottom lip. This was the moment. The tipping point where Gloria would make her decision. The decision that would alter everything.

A sister.

No sister.

Her mother finally began walking again, slowly, so she could stay connected with Amber.

"I'm glad you found her, but I fear I'm not quite ready for this."

Nobody was talking to her.

Her mother had been silent for two days and Amber hadn't dared try to broach the subject or even say hello, for fear of interrupting whatever her mom was working out in her mind.

There was nothing from Russell about the trailer--John had passed on the message about Blair days ago.

And there was nothing from Scott about whether he thought she was ready, and Amber was at a loss about how she could prove her love to him.

She had nothing, nothing, nothing.

She didn't even have waitressing to eat up her spare time, and oddly enough, she missed serving at Benny's. The place had always been like a second home to her, and the staff and regular customers like family. Working there had been similar to a homecoming once she'd gotten over her initial feeling of being overwhelmed. At Benny's she'd been an expert. She'd had authority. People took her suggestions and trusted her. She was somebody.

In the least likely of places--Blueberry Springs, as a waitress-- she had found what she'd always been seeking. Well, a good portion of it, anyway.

She still hadn't fully wrapped her head around it, but she understood why her mother had stayed. And the tips had been pretty good, too. Although part of that may have been people believing Amber had not only lost her boyfriend, but her job, too, and were trying to express their sympathy and support.

But she was still missing a piece in her understanding of herself, her life, and she didn't know how to find it. Fix it. Get what she wanted.

Scott.

Her family. Sister, father. The works.

She needed a plan. She needed…

Amber sighed.

She needed Blueberry Springs.

She didn't know what she was looking for, only that she'd likely find it in town.

Climbing into the golf cart, she turned the key. Nothing. Not even a click. It couldn't be out of gas. It had to be the battery, or the starter. She jiggled the battery connection and tried again. Still nothing. Mandy's fiancé, Frankie, had once said something about solenoid when Mandy's 4x4 refused to start. Not that Amber had any clue what that meant. Only that something had to be tapped or replaced, or required some magical mumbo-jumbo that probably involved incantations chanted with one's eyes crossed while waving a special wrench over the engine.

Which meant Amber was walking to town.

Actually, she should jog. She was rebuilding herself, right? She should exercise. Too much time in front of the keyboard wasn't good for her butt. Back in the house she changed into her favorite pair of sneakers and tied them nice and tight. It was a gorgeous day, with the meadows and hills turning green, contrasting against the rocky cliffs, and looking like something from a magazine. The clouds seemed impossibly high in the sky as she jogged down the short gravel driveway, then skipped out on to the road that led to town. So far, so good. She felt springy and spry. It was easy. She could practically see a new Amber developing as she ran. Toned arms, slim waist, and a butt to die for.

A few feet down the road she developed a stitch in her side and her breathing became jagged. She glanced back at the distance she had come. The house still looked big, barely more than a stone's throw away.

She continued along, trying to work out the cramp as her

mind flitted over all the things in her life that weren't lining up the way she wanted. A familiar panicky feeling made it harder to breathe, and she slowed to a walk before finally placing her hands on her knees and bending over, gasping.

This couldn't be her life.

It couldn't be.

She'd gone from a single child and girlfriend of a minor local celebrity to a spectacle with more family secrets than Blueberry Springs had rumors.

She began moving again at a slow trot, paying special attention to her breathing, trying to find balance. She could fix this. She could get the life she wanted. Delia had done it. So could Amber. It was within reach. Possible.

As she neared town, a vehicle pulled up alongside her. It was Mary Alice and a woman everyone knew as Gran.

"Need a ride?" Mary Alice asked, window down.

"Just walking, thanks," Amber said, trying not to sound too out of breath while doing a half jog, half walk. She probably looked as though she was trying to hustle herself to a washroom before disaster struck.

"It seems like you're in a hurry."

"Just exercising." She continued moving, attempting to seem relaxed as Mary Alice drove slowly alongside.

"I saw you on the news," Gran said. "Everyone keeps saying the book's not about you, although I found it strikingly similar. Well, except for you and Scott, of course."

Amber stopped, hands on her hips, her lungs searing with pain. "Yeah?"

"You need to make a big scene like Mandy did. No man can say no to a grand declaration of love," Gran advised, and Mary Alice nodded thoughtfully in agreement.

That could be true. The dress hadn't worked, but Jen had admitted it hadn't been a large part of her snagging Rob, either.

But Mandy had engaged in a grand act that had definitely showed Frankie the depth of her intent.

Which meant Amber needed to talk to her friend.

"Who was that woman with you the other day?" Mary Alice asked. "She looks so much like your mother did at that age."

"Long lost relative," Amber said as she picked up her speed, hoping to leave the car behind. Instead, it sped up and kept pace.

She needed to get to Blueberry Springs. Needed to pick Mandy's brain. Not get sucked into revealing gossip about herself, her mother, her life.

"Sister, perhaps?" Mary Alice asked with a pointed look.

"You should wear one of those special bras," Gran suggested. "You know, the kind that give you one boob. What are they called? Sort of smashes it all so it doesn't bounce up and give you a black eye."

"It's called a sports bra," Amber said. She turned to the car. "Can I catch a ride?"

"Will you tell me who Delia is?"

"There's nothing to tell."

Mary Alice sighed and stopped to let her in. "No point wearing out the soles of a perfectly good pair of shoes. I'll figure out who she is one way or another."

That was what Amber feared--and that her mother wasn't prepared for her secret to be exposed.

"Mary Alice, let it go. She's just a distant relative."

"Sister?" she pressed.

Amber sighed and rolled her eyes dramatically, as though Mary Alice was so off base it wasn't even worth responding.

"You need to support those girls if you're going to keep up with that thing you're doing out there, Amber Lynn," Gran continued. "They're bouncing all over the place and you're going to give yourself a brain injury."

"I think shoulder checking would give me greater danger." Amber gestured to her backside, which had been bouncing right along with her chest, and Gran let out a laugh rich with amusement.

"Drop me off at Mandy's if you can."

"One grand gesture coming up!" Mary Alice said, putting the car in gear. "If you won't tell me about your long-lost sister Delia, tell me about your mother. What happened on that trip of hers?"

"Who is Delia?" Gran asked. "I thought Amber was looking for her father. What happened to that family of yours, anyway?"

Amber sat back in the plush seat, wondering that same thing herself.

And what *had* happened on the cruise? Had her mother fallen in love with her ex once again? Or had she simply enjoyed her first trip away and was recharged from having someone else wait on her instead of the other way around?

"Looks like Gloria is in love," Mary Alice said knowingly.

If she was, it was with John. Amber found it hard to wrap her mind around that one.

If anything had happened on the cruise and her mother hadn't said anything to anyone, then that was yet another secret Amber would never unearth unless her mom was ready. And right now it seemed as though she would never be ready to show Amber her life, her past. The secrets Amber had already exposed were starting to undermine her ability to move on, get her life together and be with Scott. Instead of solving her problems, it felt as though they were only complicating them.

"I heard you hate your father," Gran said. "I don't think he's going to pop out of the woodwork if he's heard that, if you know what I'm saying."

"Not after over twenty years," Mary Alice added.

"It's okay--he doesn't live in town. And he doesn't know I'm his."

In fact, maybe he would remain a secret. Because, as Amber was beginning to understand, sometimes things *were* complicated and best not unearthed unless all parties were ready.

"MANDY?" Amber called, pushing through the glass door into her friend's restaurant. She was feeling determined after her run down the mountain. She couldn't force her mother to do anything, and even though it had been only a few weeks, she was tired of waiting to hear everything about her family, and placing her life on hold as a result.

Would it make a massive difference in her world if she knew who her father was? Probably not.

As for Delia, she had simply told her that she was working things out with their mother and would be in touch when the timing was right. And her sister had understood.

"Hey, Amber," one of Mandy's brothers, Ethan, said from behind the cash register. "Looking for my sister?"

Amber nodded, snatching a brownie from under a glass dome and leaving a few crumpled bills on the counter. She might have to wait for her mother, but she didn't have to wait for love. She would figure out how to make a grand gesture and would have her best friend, Scott, in her arms by the end of the night if it killed her.

"She's in the back doing the books," Ethan said, jerking a thumb toward the kitchen.

"Better than doing Frankie," Amber joked, heading to the swinging doors. "It would be awkward walking in on that."

Ethan shuddered in reply.

Amber found her friend working in the small office off her kitchen, forehead furrowed as she typed on her computer, glancing from time to time at the stack of papers to her left.

"Hi," Amber said. "Question for you?"

"The cost of butter? How much my electricity usage has increased in the past three months? I know the answers to those at the moment." She pushed her hair up into a loose knot on the top of her head, then released it as she sat back in her chair. "I really need a better system."

"Oh, yeah. I forgot to tell you. I have a couple of options figured out for you for keeping track of things. I'll email them, or get together if you want."

"Great. Thanks. Hey, how'd the dress go over?"

"It didn't."

"Aww." Her friend looked genuinely bothered, and Amber felt the sting of rejection as freshly as if it had happened again.

"Do you have any leftover spray paint?"

"From giving this place a makeover?" Mandy asked, moving past Amber to check the storage room. She was wearing washed-and-worn designer jeans that fitted her contours in a way that would cause Amber to sell her family secrets to the press if she could obtain the same results.

Okay, maybe not the best analogy, she thought, crossing her arms.

"Whatever you have and don't need."

Now that she was here, she didn't want to mention Mandy's grand gesture, which had led to her spray painting her declaration of love for her now-fiancé on the town's water tower. Amber had a feeling her friend would put two and two together and try to stop her. Mandy's little stunt had got her apprehended by Scott, and led to her having to repaint the entire tower. But it had also snagged Frankie's undying love.

In Amber's mind, the cost-benefit analysis came out in favor of spray painting the tower.

Mandy gave her a long look before riffling through her supply closet. "I have this." She shook a can of spray paint. "About a third left. Want it?"

Amber held the can against her chest. "Thank you."

Mandy faced her, hands on her hips. "What are you going to do with it?"

She shrugged.

"Amber Lynn!" Mandy hauled her back into her office and shut the door, making Amber feel immediately claustrophobic in the tiny space. "You had better not be planning to do what I think you're planning to do!"

"Nothing. I'm not. Nothing." She was stuttering. She was so bad at keeping secrets. No wonder everyone was already figuring out who Delia was.

"You so are!"

Amber waved, paint tucked under her arm, as she hustled out the office before her friend could change her mind for her.

"There are other ways. Ways that are legal," Mandy called after her.

Yeah, and they hadn't worked. She was desperate. She needed to do something. Take action. She couldn't live like this any longer. One more day without Scott was one day too long.

Amber strode back into the office. "Don't. Tell. Scott."

Mandy's shoulders slumped. "Having to repaint that water tower wasn't fun, Amber. If the town hadn't helped me out I'd still be up there and still picking specks of aquamarine off my skin."

"Who said anything about painting the water tower?" Amber said, a new idea blossoming in her mind.

MANDY HAD BEEN TOTALLY onto her. Well, sort of.

She had planned to spray paint her initials along with Scott's on the tower. But after talking to her friend she'd decided to paint arrows on the road, each one leading Scott closer and closer to a spot in town where Amber would be waiting with a brilliant declaration of love, and possibly roses.

But in the end, she'd lost faith in herself and had gone with the old standby--the water tower.

However, once Amber was up on the tower, with the wind

whipping down the mountainside and the town spread out below her, it seemed more like a stupid, spontaneous idea that would cause more problems than it would solve. A police officer who was applying for a promotion wouldn't hook up with a vandal. Plus everyone would know it had been her, which would leave Scott in an awkward position if he didn't arrest her. You didn't put the man you loved in a position like that.

Amber sighed, tears leaking out as she leaned against the cold metal water tank, her legs spread out in front of her on the walkway. She idly turned the spray can from end to end, making the marble inside clang as it moved. From up here she could see the shadowy forms of people walking down Main Street, pausing to chat and laugh with each other as the streetlights came on. She could see folks out in their yards, heading inside for their favorite television shows, and trailing in from bike rides and hikes through the meadow just outside of town before it grew too dark to see. On the other side of the tower, she'd be able to see up the mountain to where she lived. Her whole world was spread out in front of her, and although it wasn't very large, for the first time the idea didn't bother her as much as she thought it should.

Amber swiped at her damp cheeks as she heard the clanging of boots coming up the steel ladder that led to the walkway where she was sitting. She glanced through the opening and saw Scott powering his way up as though he climbed five-story ladders every day. His shoulders bunched and flexed under his light police jacket as he moved, his chest so broad and strong it made her long to feel it.

"Come to enjoy the view?" she asked when he wordlessly sat beside her, barely out of breath despite the speed of his ascent.

He eyed the spray can, then glanced behind them at the pristine, unpainted surface. He seemed relieved.

Amber set down the can. She'd done it. She'd thought of Scott before her own desire to be seen and heard. That had to be something.

But was it enough?

"What?" Scott asked. He was handsome, aware, and watching her in a way that made her feel seen. He would listen to whatever she needed to say because that's who he was. Her Scott.

She shifted to face him. A cool wind whipped down the mountain, stirring her hair into a cloud around her head. Her lips met Scott's and she savored the way his mouth was warm and giving--like him. As they continued he deepened the kiss, and Amber froze, uncertain whether she could keep up with him. If she could reciprocate on the same level. How could she ever be enough woman for a man such as Scott.

His hand went to her waist, and instead of shrinking back from the touch, she pressed against him, testing herself and her own limits. She trusted this man in a way she didn't trust anyone else on planet earth.

They kissed as though the world couldn't see them in the dusky evening, high up on the water tower.

Then Scott broke the kiss.

"You need someone you can trust." His voice was low, gravelly.

It almost sounded as though he was about to break up with her, but they weren't even together.

"Someone who is going to move at your speed. Who knows what you like. What you don't like. Someone who puts you at ease. Someone who loves you despite your mistakes."

She was still cradling his jaw from the kiss, but he leaned away, forcing her to release him or fall in his lap.

"What?" she whispered.

He watched her for a long moment, then gently laid kisses across her forehead in a way that was both heavy with sorrow and teasingly erotic.

"Not yet." He cupped her head near her ear, keeping her close. She looked into familiar, kind eyes, her body begging to get more of what Scott had to offer.

"Not yet?" she echoed, pressing her hands against his firm chest, wishing she could wrap them around his neck, taste his skin, and for it to be okay.

"Not yet."

Amber blinked back tears of frustration and rejection. Was he ever going to say yes? How much longer could she bear hearing *no*?

"I'm looking for a forever woman. A woman ready to commit."

Her heart stuttered and her voice left her. He wanted forever. They hadn't even done more than give each other a passionate kiss. How could he be so certain? How could he ask for more than she could offer? More than she had?

"That still makes you nervous, doesn't it?"

"Can't we just date for a while and then worry about forever later?"

He caressed her cheek in a way that sent shivers through her veins and made her body want to take up the cha-cha with his.

She'd come *this* close to kissing him on Valentine's Day, because it had felt so right to be in his arms. Scott was always there and she could barely imagine life without him. But she was scared. Scared she was going to screw it up and lose not only a boyfriend, but her best friend. Forever was a very long time and was moving faster than the speed of light.

But she'd already made him wait so long. He wanted her. They knew each other better than anyone else.

She couldn't chicken out. What if this was the only chance she got? She cleared her throat, placed her hands on Scott's waist and tipped her head up to meet his half-amused eyes. "I'm ready."

"Yeah? Then prove it."

"I've been trying!" She pushed away from him. "I was going to do this grand gesture thing up here today, but I thought of what a pain in the butt that would be for you because you'd have to arrest me. I am so sick and tired of you telling me I'm not ready, and wanting marriage before we even have a date. I can't promise you forever when we hadn't even had today. You're expecting too much from me, Scott. I can't do it. I can't give you everything because I don't even have everything."

She froze. What did that mean?

"You're an incredible friend. I'm just…" She sputtered to a halt, Scott's gaze so intense and probing it broke her heart.

"Just what?" His hands were flexed at his sides, his body coiled with something she wasn't sure she liked.

Tears were streaking down her cheeks like missiles. "I'm scared, okay?"

"Of me?"

She shook her head, picking at the pine gum stuck to the bottom of her shoe.

"Then?"

She shrugged, unable to say it, a large lump forming in her chest, making it difficult to breathe without hiccuping.

"What?" His voice was loud, echoing back over the valley.

"Of… of ruining everything. Okay?" She stood up, suddenly angry. "Of wrecking everything. Our friendship. Your reputation. I mean, look at me. Actually look at me, Scott. Not who you think I am or my potential or your fantasy of me or whatever you think you see. I'm nothing special. I screw things up. My family is one big screwed-up secret. I'm not something great and wonderful. I like Blueberry Springs. I like waitressing. I'm… I'm one step away from showing up at bingo with curlers in my hair. I'll never be mayor. I'm the kind of person boyfriends make fun of in books. I can't… I just…" Amber choked up, feeling so empty and worthless and hurt that she couldn't even begin to process everything swirling up within her like a muddy lake bottom in a storm. She collapsed onto the metal walkway with a clang, sobbing as every worthless feeling inside broke free.

She covered her face, embarrassed at the way she was ugly crying in front of the man she had planned to woo. She didn't know whether to be mad at him for giving her space and not comforting her, or relieved.

"They say what doesn't kill you makes you stronger," she sniffed through her tears, "but I sure don't feel any stronger."

"You're also not dead," he said, carefully placing himself beside her so they were shoulder to shoulder. "That's something, right?"

She let out a choked laugh, mopping her face with the sleeve of her sweatshirt.

"You're even leaving," she said. "Leaving the town you love. Leaving me. How can you ask for forever when you're not staying?"

"Aren't you leaving?" His voice was gentle.

Stupid Blueberry Springs. Of course she wasn't leaving. The town had her hooked. She'd served her first burger, and now she was stuck here forever. It had lured her into its comforting familiarity, and now the idea of moving back to the city, of being a stranger who didn't matter, felt exhausting and chilling.

"I've always been honest about where I stand on that matter," she said, not wanting to let him be right. "I'm not going to change."

She'd tried and had failed.

"I happen to like you the way you are."

"No you don't!" she exploded. "You want me to change. You say I'm not ready, and all this other mumbo-jumbo, instead of wanting me the way I am." She stood, yelling at him, not caring if anyone in the park below could hear her. "I want a man who is proud of me, proud to be by my side and tell everyone that he loves me just the way I am. Who isn't secretly trying to make me into something else. I'm not anyone else. I'm me. I'm Amber and I serve a purpose. I'm important."

Scott's expression became unreadable. "I never asked you to change. I only want you to come to me when you're ready. Ready to be mine until the end of time. You can never brush your hair again and I'll still love you, still want you as mine. But you have to be ready, Amber. You have to be ready in here."

He pointed to her heart.

"And until you can say the words I need to hear, you're not."

Darn him. Darn him and his perfect lines crumbling her inner bad mood. Darn him for always being right.

He gently placed a kiss on her lips, which brought her falling against him, trying to get closer, willing the tingles that seared her skin to never stop, but to keep building as she knew they would. As they would only with a man like Scott. Only Scott.

He broke away and she said, "You are one steamy guy, Officer Malone, and if there is one thing I do in this life it will be to prove to you that I am ready."

His gaze burned and he grasped her chin between his thumb and forefinger. He stared at her with an intensity that made her feel as though there could never be any secrets between them. That he saw the truth--she did love him, even if she couldn't say the words.

He blinked, breaking the spell. "You don't even own curlers and you don't play bingo."

She lifted her chin, jerking free. "I could buy curlers. Maybe those fuzzy ones I've seen Mary Alice wear while walking her dog."

"But you won't." His gaze was smoldering again. "I won't let you."

"Try and stop me."

His look took her breath away as he snatched her hand, pushing it above her head against the water tank. Then he kissed her in a way that made her think maybe he *had* seen all of her all this time, and maybe, just maybe, he still loved her. And all she had to do was find that secret piece that would put them together.

Forever.

8

*A*mber was a mess. Scott had kissed her like crazy there against the water tower, then let her go.

She'd lain awake all night thinking about him, his kisses, and how she wanted more. A lot more.

Amber paced around her yard, wondering how on earth she was going to find a version of herself that was ready to dive into forever without even a first date. She trusted Scott, loved him. But there was still something about herself that prevented her from saying those three little words. They were so simple.

"I love you, I love you, I love you."

Simple. Easy. And completely unavailable when she needed them the most.

She needed to figure it out.

And then there was her mother. Amber was getting nowhere there, either.

She sat on her front step, inhaling the fresh mountain air. She would miss the way mornings smelled in Blueberry Springs if she went back to Dakota. The quiet. The peacefulness. The way she'd see bears walking down the road, toward town to find garbage to munch on before the berries ripened.

Bear.

Amber scrambled to flatten her back against the closed door behind her, not moving, even though the animal was well over two hundred feet away. She'd never liked the fact that bears sometimes came into town. When they did it usually meant the berries weren't ready and they were looking for other meal options.

Such as Amber.

Pulling her phone out of her back pocket, she quickly texted Scott, alerting him about the situation. The idea of him having to deal with the wild animal sent her heart racing. Bears tended to be fairly predictable, and Rob Raine--Jen's boyfriend--would likely be doing most of the bear herding. But Amber knew Scott would be backing him up, trying to chase the bear out of town.

Was this love--a deep-seated fear that something would happen to Scott and she wouldn't have the chance to tell him how she felt?

A familiar tightness gripped her vocal cords at the thought of expressing how she felt. What would it take to be able to tell him?

Maybe finding her sister and her father *were* the missing pieces. Maybe it did matter more than she'd realized. Maybe knowing them would help her get over this feeling inside that she wasn't enough, help her understand herself better. It seemed ridiculous to depend on someone else to figure out what she needed to fix, but she was out of ideas again.

The dress and the grand gesture had belly flopped. All that was left was being herself.

Which would be easy if she knew who she was. If she knew where she had come from. If she understood how it all fit together.

And there was only one person who could help her with that.

Her mother.

Realizing that she had no car, no golf cart, and a bear was in the middle of the road, Amber groaned. She was trapped.

Sighing, she climbed into her car, hoping for a miracle. She fished the keys from above the visor and held her breath as she cranked the engine, keeping her forehead against the steering wheel as the motor turned over, first try.

She sat up, staring out the dusty windshield at the town nestled in the valley below. Blueberry Nosy-Rosy Springs. Someone must have fixed her car, because no amount of sitting would have cured the shudder it had had just before it died.

She grinned.

"I love you, Blueberry Springs. See? I can say it. Love, love, love."

Maybe her life wasn't what she wanted it to be yet. Maybe it wasn't as exciting as she had dreamed it could be. But it wasn't so bad, either. She didn't need a lot to be happy, so maybe she simply needed to stop trying to chase dreams that weren't her own, and start loving it.

***

"Mom?" Amber walked through the house, searching for her.

"I'm out back," Gloria called.

Amber joined her on the patio, where she was tending to her garden--everything in pots so she could bring it in on cool days and nights up here in the mountains, thereby extending the season. When she saw Amber's expression, she rocked back on her heels.

Amber sat on the edge of the patio, hugging her legs against her chest. "I'm going to visit Delia on the weekend," she said. "Would you like to meet her?"

Her mother studied the lettuce in front of her, plucking a dried leaf. "Is she... What's she like?"

"She's really nice." Amber held her breath as her mom watched her for a long moment, deciding.

"Okay."

"Okay, you'll meet her?" Amber let go of her legs and stood. She could barely believe it was that easy. All she'd had to do was ask. It seemed too simple.

"I figure if all of Blueberry Springs has met her, then I probably should, too."

Amber hesitated, wondering how far she should push. Should she take the success and run with it, or could she ask about her father, as well?

Life was short.

It was her right to know. What was the worst that could happen?

"Can I meet my dad, too?" Amber gave her mom a playful look in hopes of easing the bluntness of her question.

"Don't push it, Amber Lynn. The last thing I need is you running around town trying to figure out who he is. It's bad enough that you have everyone thinking you hate the man. Word is going to get back to him, if it hasn't already, you know."

"I thought he didn't know who I was?"

Her mother's lips turned white as she pressed them together. "He doesn't."

"Then why would you say that?"

"He's not a stupid man."

"So he does know who I am, even though you lied to him?"

"Nobody wants to think they are hated. I raised you better than that."

"I thought you said he didn't live in town."

"I never said that."

Amber sat on the edge of the patio once again. Her father knew who she was and lived in town. He had seen her grow up and hadn't stepped forward. He didn't want her as part of his family. She had disappointed him somehow.

The thought brought tears to her eyes and she jumped to her feet again, heading back into the house.

"Amber?" her mother called, worry lacing her voice.

She needed to get out of here, but couldn't stop the tears from falling. It had felt so freeing, thinking that her father hadn't rejected her. That there was a possibility he might still want her in his life even though she was an adult.

"Amber." Her mother caught up with her at the door, since she was unable to leave without showing the town that she was bawling her face off. "Oh, Amber. I am so sorry."

"He knows who I am and hasn't stepped forward?"

"Oh, honey. I wish it were simpler. He's just trying to respect my wishes. I did what I thought was best for everyone."

"Tell him I want to meet him," Amber pleaded. "We're all adults. Please, Mom. I just want to know."

"Amber, it will change everything."

She had thought knowing who her father was no longer mattered, but was beginning to feel as though he was the one thing that mattered most.

"Then maybe it's time for change." Amber gently shut the door behind her as she fled her mother's house.

AMBER PARKED her car in front of Mandy's restaurant. She was early for the meet-up where she would introduce her mother and sister to each other.

She had barely spoken to her mom since the blowup about her father, and wasn't sure if Gloria had talked to him or not. But as if to make a point, her mother had suggested she meet Delia in Blueberry Springs. And in a public venue, no less.

Amber wasn't sure what it meant, but hoped to know soon. It was ten minutes to eight and the café was quiet, other than the odd tourist having a late supper. Except her mother was already there. As was Delia. They had already met and were sitting head to head, chatting over the table that separated them, sharing one of Mandy's huge whiskey-and-gumdrop brownies.

Amber stood in the doorway, not quite believing her eyes. She had trusted Delia. Had thought nobody could ever replace her in her mother's eyes. But there they were. Acting as though they had known each other for years.

She almost turned to flee, feeling as though she was a third wheel, but her mother--*their* mother--spotted her and waved her over, smiling.

Amber gave her a hug, even though it wasn't her usual thing when they'd seen each other recently. She had a suspicion that sibling rivalry was providing the deep-seated urge to claim ownership over her mother, as though it was a competition. As though she had to flaunt in Delia's face that she was first in their mom's thoughts and heart.

She didn't like acting this way, and definitely didn't like the feelings storming around inside her like a bad case of indigestion.

"You two have met?" Amber said, stating the obvious as she sat down.

"It's as though we've known each other all of our lives. It's incredible," Delia stated, forking more brownie into her mouth.

She looked so happy that Amber felt bad for not wanting to share their mom. But she wanted Gloria all to herself. Delia already had a mother, and didn't need two. Three, if you counted her mother-in-law. She was flush with mothers. She also had two dads--she'd met her biological father through the government adoption database already--plus she had a father-in-law. Amber had one parent. One. And Delia, her sister, was honing in on her.

A red haze flashed in front of Amber's eyes, and she feared she was going to say something rash. She needed to get a grip on the anger ripping through her.

But seeing the two so cozy...

Breathe, Amber. It's okay. Your mom still loves you.

"I'm going to go get a brownie," she said, wondering for a second if they would tell her to simply grab a third fork and share with them. They didn't.

She went to the counter and ordered one, handing Ethan her money.

"Is she a cousin?" he asked, placing change in her palm.

"She's related, yes." Amber still didn't know if her mother was letting the Delia secret out or not.

"She seems cool. A lot like you."

"Yeah. Just like me." Only better. More exciting.

Amber headed back to the table, focusing on her treat instead of the way her sister and mother were talking a mile a minute with no attempts to include her.

"Sorry I was late," she said. "I thought we said eight."

Her mom patted her hand, not looking away from Delia, who was asking about Gloria's personal history and how she'd met Delia's father. Amber feared her mother would clam up at the mention of her old high school boyfriend, but instead she smiled at Delia and said, "Anything you want to know, just ask. There are no secrets."

"Do people know who Delia is?" Amber interjected. "Or is *that* still a secret?" She knew she was giving her mother tone, but couldn't help it. She was fed up with the mysteries and the stingy delving out of information. How could Gloria offer to tell Delia everything when Amber was still receiving so little? And why was Amber's father a bigger secret compared to an entire secret child? A secret child whose father had sought her out despite abandoning her before birth.

"Are you okay?" her mother asked.

"I'm fine. So?" Amber crossed her arms. "Can I tell people I have a sister? Or do I have to keep lying to the town and dodging questions so that you can keep having your big secrets?"

"Amber!" her mother scolded, darting a glance at Delia, who looked uncomfortable.

"Would you like a few minutes?" Delia asked.

"No, it's okay. I'm leaving." Amber stood up, catching a glimpse of Frankie walking toward Mandy, his gait slow and patient. As the couple kissed their hellos Amber squeezed her hands into fists, fighting for control. Friends to lovers. Just one more thing she couldn't have.

She picked up her purse and turned, just about slamming into a man about her height.

"Oops." John Abcott steadied her, smiling at Amber's mom. "Hello, Gloria." He placed one hand on the back of the vacant chair beside Delia. "Mind if I join you?"

Gloria blushed, her palm on her chest as she gave a small shoulder lift of acquiesce, and Amber just about stopped breathing. They were back together.

"Tell me about the cruise," Amber said, not quite ready to leave, but not quite ready to stay. "You were on the same ship?"

"We were," John said, still smiling at Gloria, who was all but preening and giving flirty looks. Amber had never seen her act that way.

Her mom was in love with John Abcott.

He'd been through two wives.

He had a daughter.

He was a lawyer. Her mother was a waitress.

But they'd dated when they were younger. Before she'd dated Philip the second time.

No, no. The connections didn't fit.

There was no reason for them to date secretively.

It was my idea to date secretly, as he needed his family's support. Getting a law degree wasn't cheap.

He was starting a business. Legal office.

He's successful.

He came from a different world.

Hello.

Amber fell into the chair she'd vacated, her mind spinning, knocking threads of old conversations together like a high-speed jigsaw puzzle.

But John had always been so accepting of everyone. It was

difficult to think of him as judging her mother so harshly. Of them breaking up over a secret baby that wasn't even his.

He had his own family by then. A wife. A kid on the way.

His daughter, Marisa, had been in the same grade as her.

"When did you start your business?" Amber whispered.

John watched her for a moment, a sad look in his eyes as he contemplated his answer. And she knew. Right there. Right then.

John Abcott was her father. He *had* known. He'd always been there, looking out for her. Sponsoring soccer. Coaching her team. Joining her for vodka and peanuts.

He had been a father figure in her life because he *was* her father.

He hadn't rejected her, only accepted her and helped her in the ways he could, while respecting Gloria's wishes.

But Amber had hurt him. She had lashed out like a spoiled teenager and told the town she hated him.

She tried to whisper an apology, her vision narrowing as the force of the knowledge hit her hard in the chest. She gripped the edge of the table so she wouldn't topple out of her chair, and tried to force herself to glance up at her mother, to look for confirmation.

A warm, strong hand gripped her shoulder. "I think you need some fresh air," said a familiar voice. It wasn't her father. It was Scott.

He whisked her away from the table before anyone could protest. Instead of taking her to the front door and out onto the Main Street sidewalk, he pulled her through the kitchen area, waving away Mandy, who looked up in concern as they passed.

Scott closed the steel door behind them, leading her down the alley's uneven asphalt, around potholes filled with murky rainwater, before finally pushing her against a brick wall behind a dumpster.

"You okay?" he asked.

She shivered and wrapped her arms around herself. Was John

really her father? Was she just grasping at straws, wishing for him to be?

But the look in his eyes. His expression. The things he'd done in their shared history. It all lined up.

And her mother loved him. They smiled at each other in a way that said something.

Amber looked nothing like John. Because she looked so much like Gloria.

Scott pulled off his police jacket, draping it over her shoulders. It was surprisingly heavy, the thick and sturdy material weighing her down, grounding her. She pulled it closer, savoring the warmth from Scott's body, as well as his scent.

He said nothing, but his gaze stayed on hers.

"I think John is my father," Amber said, feeling silly as she said it out loud.

"I think so, too."

She looked up so quickly the barrette holding back her bangs slipped out of place. "What?"

"I think he is."

"How long have you known?"

"A few years. But everyone figured it was Philip. Then when John divorced again and didn't step forward, I decided it was probably best to keep my thoughts to myself."

"What do I do? What do I say?"

"Nothing."

Amber thought about that for a moment. "Nothing?"

"Nothing."

She had to say something to her mother. Had to. She couldn't let this one sit around, waiting for her mother to be ready.

Amber shrugged out of Scott's jacket, handing it to him, shivering when their fingers produced jolts of electricity at the touch. She already missed his jacket's comfort and heat, wishing she could wrap herself in him.

"Scott?"

"Yeah?"

"Will I ever be ready?" She placed her palms against his chest, needing the security that only he could give. "For us? For forever?" Her voice cracked on "forever" and she hated that she wasn't stronger. That she wasn't yet the woman Scott needed her to be. It felt as though every step she took to bring them closer did the opposite. She felt crushed and broken, and wished she was more. So much more.

He wrapped his hands around hers, bringing them to his lips for a light kiss. "You may not feel as though you are first in there right now." He tipped his head toward the café they'd abandoned. "But you'll always be first in here." He pulled her hands over his heart. "Always."

WHOEVER SAID BEING the youngest meant having privileges was so full of crap.

All anyone in town wanted to do was talk about her sister. Yes, Amber got it. Her sister was new and exciting even for the non-gossips. A long-lost daughter that no one had known about. Surprise!

But the worst was that her mother was just as absorbed in her long-lost daughter as everyone else was. She kept asking Amber if she was okay, and what was she supposed to say? "No, I'm feeling replaced, jealous, and am having a difficult time dealing with sharing you--my only parent?" She needed to suck it up. Grow up. Get over it.

What she really wanted to do was ask if John was truly her father. Amber was freaking out, not knowing what to do, say, or how to act.

She needed to focus on what she did have. She'd always wanted a sibling and now she had one. Delia was wonderful and wanted to be a part of her life. And her mother had accepted her, as well. It was completely natural that the two of them wanted to spend time together.

So after her poor behavior at Mandy's café, Amber had felt the need to make it up to her mother. To prove to her and Delia that she really was okay with this new relationship despite her insecurities, but also to show her mom that she could handle tough situations. If she pulled that off, then maybe her mother would confirm whether John was her father or not.

And now, instead of watching a matinee in the local theater, Amber was serving tables at Benny's while her mother and Delia went on a hike through Blueberry Springs's beautiful meadows, laughing and bonding. Which kind of made Amber feel like a forgotten stepchild.

"Amber?" called Elsie Nagorski, a resident of the local nursing home who came to Benny's for the Tuesday night special more often than not. She was seated by the window so she could "see the gossip go by" with her visiting sister. "Come over and meet my sister, Wilma Star. She lives--"

"In Windermere, Ontario, right? Muskoka? I remember. Nice to see you again."

"Are you still playing soccer?" asked Mrs. Star. The last time she'd come to visit, Amber had been about twelve and had been practicing for a tournament. She was impressed the woman still remembered her, let alone that she'd played soccer.

"No, no." Amber held her order pad and pen poised, hoping that they wouldn't get into where her life had taken her since their last meeting.

"She was in a book," Elsie said.

And there it was.

"That's terribly exciting." Mrs. Star smiled. "Did you hear about the excitement in my neck of the woods?"

Amber shook her head, realizing it would be some time before the women were ready to order. The sisters were always making bets and trying to outdo each other, and she had a feeling this conversation would only serve to highlight that.

She hoped she and Delia never got to that point. Although not having grown up together might help the competition aspect--that was, if Amber got over her jealousy.

"Hailey Summer, my friend's daughter—you remember her? She came out here a few summers ago."

Elsie and Amber nodded.

"Well, she's dating--"

"Finian Alexander, the movie star," Elsie said, fidgeting with her cutlery, obviously feeling outdone. "I lost that bet, but you lost the one over who started the Blueberry Springs forest fires."

"I was thousands of miles away! How was I to know it wasn't Jen? All I had to go on were the things you told me, as well as the newspapers."

"And I was thousands of miles away when you started in about Finian Alexander checking out your garden gnomes."

"Ladies," Amber interrupted.

"Oh, it's okay." Elsie patted her gray bun, adjusting a wisp of hair that was out of place. "Just a little sibling rivalry. You'll get used to it." To her sister, she added, "Amber just found her long-lost sister last week."

Mrs. Star looked up, her eyes alight. "Oh, that is terribly exciting."

"It is. So, today's specials are--"

"We already know what we want," Elsie said, ordering for both of them.

"You can't go wrong with our burgers," Amber said.

"Unless you have dentures," Elsie laughed, popping hers out and waving them around before putting them back into place.

Amber shuddered at the unexpected reveal. "I'll make sure to bring you a knife and fork."

Scrawling in her notepad as she walked between tables, she spotted John entering the restaurant.

Dad?

She was going to have a heck of a time acting natural around him. She didn't know for certain, but as their eyes connected, she knew that John believed he was her father, too.

He quickly took a table by the door, and Amber couldn't help but wonder if he'd been hoping to see Gloria.

Amber took extra time placing the sisters' order, then collecting cutlery and a menu for John.

What would he order for supper? Did he favor the cheese-and-basil pizza, too? Would he want a vodka shot as he did when they hung out at Brew Babies? How many times had the two of them sat elbow to elbow at the bar, knocking back a shot and eating peanuts while shooting the breeze? With her father.

As she walked to his table, half wishing there was another waitress on tonight, she studied him with fresh eyes. Amber had her mother's long fingers. Her eyes, her chin. She looked a lot like Gloria, just as Delia did. However, John had a slight cowlick to the left just like she did. She studied his ears as she set down his cutlery, wishing she could remember what her own ears looked like.

"You figured it out, didn't you?" John said with a slight smile.

"Sounds like you did, too?"

"I've always wondered, despite what your mother said. But in Mandy's the other night it was like a light bulb went off. There can't be any other explanation."

"My mom doesn't know I figured it out," Amber said in a whisper, knowing that others were likely eavesdropping--as they always did.

"She hasn't said anything?" he asked in surprise.

"No. You?"

"Never. Liked to chase me away whenever I broached the topic," he said in a low voice. He looked up from studying the menu. "What's on tap tonight?"

"No shot? Benny has several brands of vodka."

"I'm planning on having the new burger. The California something-or-other? I thought maybe a beer would go nicely with it."

"We carry Brew Babies pale ale and it's been popular with the burger." The fact that he wasn't ordering vodka left her feeling inexplicably hollow and as though their shared shots and companionship hadn't been real. She realized now just how important his company had been to her.

"Sounds good. I'll take a pint."

The usual joy that came with customers accepting her recommendations didn't arrive. He was being so official, a proper customer. Not warm or casual. He was putting up barriers.

Was he trying to make sure other diners wouldn't pick up a hint in his body language? Or maybe he'd solved the mystery and now the reality of having her as his daughter didn't seem so bright and shiny.

Amber half wondered if this was how he'd acted when Gloria had told him about Delia. Just slowly withdrawn and shut her out. Suddenly, John as her mother's dismissive ex-boyfriend, the man Amber disliked for his treatment of her mom, didn't seem quite so impossible.

Amber glanced at the neighboring tables, ensuring that customers weren't trying to get her attention, and said, "I can see it in the way my mom looks at you that she never got over you. She had no other viable choice when Delia was born. She was a teenager with a crappy home life and no education. You decimated her with your actions, your words. She is a strong, capable, kind, and caring woman who did a fine job of raising me." Amber rested her fingers on the tabletop, leaning close enough to whisper, "So whatever happens and whatever you choose to do, don't you dare judge her again and make her regret everything good she's done for her daughters."

John froze, and for a moment Amber thought he'd had a stroke, he was so still.

"Okay," he said with a nod, looking at her with a mix of pride and surprise. "Okay."

She straightened her spine, realizing that she was strong enough to say what she needed to say. Strong enough to stand up for the people in her life who mattered most. Strong enough to help right a past mistake.

"I was the one in the wrong, not your mother." John's hands slowly closed into fists, his eyes growing stormy. "I was so focused on myself and my career that I did and said some very hurtful things. I'm not proud of who I was or how I acted." His voice was getting louder and he quickly lowered it again. "Your mother was very brave. I betrayed her trust." His eyes filled with moisture and Amber realized he'd likely been kicking himself for a very long time, and had probably been trying to make amends in any way he could. "I was a fool. If I'd stood up to my parents things would have been different. So different."

"You wouldn't have Marisa." Amber pressed her hand over his, silencing him. There was no point walking the what-if road. It only led to dark caves and forests with gnarly looking trees that left you so unsettled you couldn't sleep at night.

"The past is the past," she said. "I'm staying in Blueberry Springs. There is plenty of time to talk about the future, if that's what you'd like to focus on."

She was staying.

She was staying!

She needed to talk to Scott. She needed to stop him from leaving.

John nodded, his composure back, and Amber focused on her job, not running off after the man she wanted to spend the rest of her life with.

"I'd like that," John said, clearing his throat, pulling it together. And in that moment, Amber realized that he needed her just as much as she'd always thought she'd needed him.

"You can't leave Blueberry Springs." Amber felt desperate, but she sucked in her courage, placing her hands on her hips to show she meant business.

Scott looked up from his desk, a mechanical pencil poised between his large fingers. "That's something I normally say to people who are part of an ongoing investigation."

"In the name of love, I am telling you not to leave town."

"Love?"

"Shut up. I have a speech and you're throwing me off. I already had to wait for Dispatch to take a smoke break so I could do this in private."

He gestured for her to continue.

"Stay. Don't take a job somewhere else. Blueberry Springs is home. For you. For me. I'm not going anywhere and I don't think you should, either."

Scott leaned back, quiet for the longest moment. Finally, the corner of his lips lifted into a smile. "Want to know a secret?"

Amber flopped into the chair across from him in an exasperated heap. "No." He was supposed to sweep her into his arms, see that she was ready.

He played with his pencil, clicking it, then pushing the lead back in by pressing it against his muscular thigh, watching her. "I applied out so I could move to the city when you did. But I pulled my name from the application pool a few days ago."

She groaned in frustration. Why didn't he speak the same language she did? Blunt and straightforward.

Right now he was supposed to be pulling her close, kissing her, loving her. Not speaking in riddles, where she had to wait to find out what he meant. Because him withdrawing his name could mean one of two things: either he'd figured she was going to stay, so he would, too, or he'd decided she wasn't worth moving for.

"I had a feeling there would be a reason to stay."

He came around the desk.

She perked up. "Such as?"

"Stand up." Scott's voice was gruff and commanding.

She complied, and he gently slipped his fingers across her jaw before tangling them in her loose locks. Her head tilted toward his involuntarily as he angled his mouth, drawing them close. He stopped an inch from meeting her lips, his breath soft on her cheek.

This was where it all happened. It all came together.

She met his gaze, and worlds and history passed between them. For years she'd denied his true feelings, pushed him aside and made him feel as though he wasn't good enough to be more than a friend. She'd dismissed him, as well as herself and her true feelings. She'd allowed fear to hold her back. She'd allowed herself to feel as though she wasn't enough for a man like Scott.

She'd taken his warmth, kindness, and love for granted for too long.

She brought her lips to his, erasing the distance that she'd placed between them over the years, savoring the heat of him melting into her as their kiss deepened. His hand wrapped around her wrist bound her in place as she brought her free hand up to his hard chest, then around his shoulder to the back of his neck. Wide, strong, and vulnerable.

She was kissing her best friend as only lovers did. It was no quick peck as love passed between them. They crossed the friendship line, and she hoped she'd never find herself on the other side ever again. Not with Scott.

His kisses turned commanding, his hands taking her in, one holding her close around her waist as she arched into him, the other caressing her breast. Longing and need hit her like a tropical storm and her kisses became frantic as she tried to consume him, as though this was her last kiss on planet earth.

He felt so *right*. Her whole body was alive and in command of her moves.

Kissing one's best friend was definitely not overrated. At least if your best friend was Scott Malone, hunk extraordinaire.

She finally broke free, her breath coming in desperate bursts. The need for more darkened his eyes and it was as though all the pent-up love he'd held within him for the past decade was bursting out. His lips were suddenly on hers again, bruising and demanding in ways she'd never dreamed of reciprocating, but craved so strongly she felt like a satellite, stuck in his orbit. She could come to depend on kisses like Scott's.

As they finally broke free again, he whispered, "You kiss like you've been wanting to do that for years." His slow, teasing grin made her heart take up an unsteady rhythm, and she opted for a sassy reply to keep the playing field fair.

"And here I kissed you just the other day. How forgettable was that, hmm?"

She'd eased out of his arms and he pulled her back with sudden speed, his lips once again hungry on hers. A gal could get used to this. No more Mr. Nice Guy Friend. Scott was a secret alpha any woman would be lucky to have.

"Don't toy with me, Amber," he said a long moment later. She'd never felt so wanted as she did in his arms. He knew everything that was wrong with her. Every flaw. Every insecurity. Every awful stupid spontaneous embarrassing thing that had ever come out of her mouth. And yet he still chose her.

The world was full of unsolved mysteries, but this was surely one of the biggest. One she hoped was never solved.

"Scott?" she asked, placing a finger against his lips before he could pull her in for another smooch. "Why do you love me?"

"I'll answer that when you're ready to tell me the same," he replied.

"I'll tell you everything," she promised, giving him a light kiss that had her desperately wanting more. "But I'm not sure you're ready for me yet."

He pulled her into a heavy kiss that left the strength in her legs waning. Under her palm she could feel his heart beating, steady and strong. Reliable.

"Amber Thompson, you're a big tease."

"I'll show you I'm not." She went to say the words that were on the tip of her tongue.

I love you. They were there, but her throat was heavy. Her head spinning.

He loved her. He was staying in his hometown for her. She wasn't leaving.

They were going to be here in Blueberry Springs. Forever.

Once she said those three big words there would be no turning back. She was locking herself into a life. Here. With one man. Forever. She'd never be someone else. She'd never…

She couldn't do it. She wasn't ready. She was still one step away.

She rested her forehead against Scott's, wanting him so badly her fingers dug into his shoulders, afraid to let go and yet so afraid to say yes, so afraid to trust her heart and the words it was whispering.

I love you, Scott. Now and forever.

9

*A*mber hurried down Main Street, hoping to catch her mother on her walk home from her early shift at Benny's.

"Amber!" Liz called as she popped out of the town office. "Wait up!"

Amber complied and Liz, wrapped in a fuzzy robin's-egg-blue pashmina, hurried to her side.

"Do you know if John's heard back from Russell?" Amber asked.

"Nothing yet as far as I know. So, how's the new sister?"

"Good."

"I heard she and your mom are inseparable."

"Yeah."

"You must feel left out."

"They have a lot to catch up on." She pointed toward the town office, hoping to move away from what was still a tender subject--and one she didn't want to be part of the local gossip. "How is Nicola doing? Did she talk to Jen about helping her with tours?"

"She'll be leading the one-hour nature hikes on Saturdays."

"Great. Well, I've got to catch up with Mom." Amber hustled away before Liz could pump her for gossip, just about slamming into Russell. Her ex was looking uncomfortable as he shifted on the sidewalk, glancing every so often over his shoulder.

Amber went to move around him, but he caught her arm. "Amber, I need to talk to you."

"Yeah? Do it through my lawyer." For whatever reason, right now she wished she could add "my dad." A lawyer dad would definitely give a girl a certain level of protection.

"Please. I need to talk to you."

Now there was a tone she hadn't been expecting.

"I'm busy. You should have called ahead."

"I figured you'd say no."

"You're not as dumb as you seem, then. You just act that way. Good to know." She started to move away, but he caught her arm again. How could she have ever been so needy as to want the affections of a man such as Russell? How could she not have seen--correction, how could she have ignored--how selfish and self-centered he was? Because she was certain he wasn't here for any reason other than himself.

"Why are you here?" she asked, not caring if she had an edge to her voice.

"I wanted to see you."

"Why? Did your editor already dump you?"

Russell couldn't look her in the eye.

"Right. You were never the man of my dreams, Russell, and I wasted a year of my life trying to convince myself otherwise." She began walking away, shooing off Fran, who had come to the door of her boutique to make sure Amber was okay.

"I wanted to apologize," Russell said, his voice carrying down the street.

She stopped cold. Those were the last words she'd ever expected to hear. She turned. Russell was staring at the display in Fran's window as though he hadn't said a word.

"Usually when a man apologizes he explains why. Here are some starting places, if you're at a loss. Cheating on me, using me, betraying me, my confidence, and our intimacy. Making me feel as though I never meant anything to you, making me a public spectacle, starting a multitude of rumors about me in my own hometown, slandering me in a libelous way, lying to me…" She had been moving closer with every word and was now in his face. "Would you like me to go on?" she asked coolly.

Russell looked at her in wonder. "You're different."

"Angrier? More jaded? Yeah, go figure on that one, huh?"

"No. More… you."

"What's that supposed to mean?"

She was taken off guard by the way he was studying her. It wasn't as though she was a bug under a seven-year-old's microscope, it was more as though he was intrigued by what he saw, and wanted to see more. The only man who had ever looked at her that way before was Scott. However, with Scott it was comforting. She knew he was looking beneath her layers and possibly seeing something good that she couldn't see in herself. But with Russell it made her feel judged and exposed.

"You're closer to the Amber I wrote about."

"So you do admit it!" She pointed at him in triumph.

"You were my muse—you knew that. That's why we came back here."

"Why we came back?" He was making no sense. He'd told her he'd liked the quiet of Blueberry Springs.

"This was the only place where you'd relax, open up and let me in."

"Here? In Blueberry Springs?"

"We'd go back to the city and you'd harden. You'd try to guess what I wanted you to say."

"No, I didn't."

Why would she have been different at home? She'd hated it and wanted out. She understood now that this town was where she belonged, but she hadn't felt that way until recently. And while it was true that in the city she had always been trying to be someone cool and sophisticated, she hadn't realized that she'd been a completely different person at home. Maybe that was why, when she decided to stay in Blueberry Springs, she'd felt a rush of relief--not just because it was easy and familiar, but because she could be herself and be accepted for that reason. There was no one to impress. Everyone knew her flaws, her problems, and they rolled with it.

"I had to figure out why you were real here. It was compelling. You are compelling." Russell touched her elbow and she shifted away, clutching the neck of her jacket. He sounded genuine, but she wasn't sure she liked where he was going with the conversation.

"You are every woman in North America. I wanted to see that. Take that. Build on it."

The book was about her, but theirs was a battle that would go nowhere. He'd backtrack in court and, as John had said, it would become a case of he said, she said. Russell would make up something that sounded good and that would be that.

And in the end, it didn't matter. People would believe what they chose to believe. Amber knew who she was, and so did those who meant the most to her. She was enough for them just the way she was and nobody, especially Russell, could come in and change that.

"It's a compliment, Amber. Did the new you learn to accept one?"

She continued to think, ignoring his digs to get her going.

"You're quiet," he said.

"I don't have anything nice to say." The man was as trustworthy as a rickety rope bridge stretched across the mouth of a jagged canyon.

"Are you plotting my death?" he asked wryly.

"Yeah, because I want to get arrested--I look great in orange jumpsuits, in case you didn't know that," Amber said absently.

Russell laughed. "I'm glad we can joke."

"Don't take my jokes as me saying everything is okay, because it's not. It's really not. What you did was unkind and unfair."

"I'm sorry."

"No, I don't think you are. The tears have already fallen, Russell. It's too little, too late."

"The book was a gift and you're obviously already over it. Cry me a river, babe."

"I'll get you a life jacket so you don't drown."

"Look below Ember's surface." Russell was raising his voice, angry with her for not being the weak, easy-to-sway woman he'd dated only weeks ago. "She's tough, resilient, confident. She is unafraid. She's bold. She goes after what she wants and makes the best of crappy situations. That's supposed to be you. I wanted to tell you that. I wanted to make sure you were okay. I wanted you to know that I saw those traits in you and that I hoped you could do something with it. Something positive."

Amber felt tears prick her eyes as scenes from Russell's book flashed through her mind. Ember *was* tough. Resilient and confident and all those things Amber had wished she was, and was on her way to becoming. But it wasn't because of him or his book. It was because she had the undying love and support of people like her mother and Scott.

Russell would not take credit for who she was. Not now. Not ever.

"You were a rotten boyfriend, Russell, so you just keep on telling yourself whatever you need to hear to make yourself feel better about the way you betrayed the woman who'd had your back. You are not the kind of person who could ever look out for me, protect me, or take care of me in the way I deserve. So don't rewrite history, *babe*. I was over you the moment your trailer went over the side of the cliff."

She began storming away, but turned and stomped back for one final blow. "And I will not pay for that 'writing cave,' as you called it. I doubt you had anything in it, and I did you a favor by getting rid of it. If anything, you should be paying me--your muse whose life you used without permission--half of your royalties."

Russell's mouth opened, then he closed it with a glare.

"Right. So we're close enough to even, and done with each other. Wish your next girlfriend good luck from me." Amber blew him a haughty kiss and sauntered down the street, high-fiving Liz, who had been eavesdropping on the whole conversation and was grinning like a mad fool.

Amber straightened her spine, realizing that she *was* someone--the someone she'd always wanted to be. She was strong enough. Smart enough. Confident enough.

She was finally enough.

She had a mother, a sister, a town, and a really fine best friend. She might not be super wealthy or put together like Delia, but she helped people and made a difference in their lives, even if only on a small scale. She didn't intentionally hurt others and her mother was proud of her. *She* should be proud of her.

And she should finally feel able to tell the man of her dreams that she loved him with all her heart.

***

"I saw Russell in town today. Did he bother you?" Scott asked. His arms were crossed and his brow lowered as though he was a bull about to charge if given the smallest inkling that there might be a threat.

They were sitting on the walkway of the water tower, enjoying the view and sharing a massive sandwich from Mandy's, along with brownies for dessert.

"No. Why didn't you warn me before I wasted a year on him?"

Scott scowled at her and she hugged him to her, warm and tight, kissing him to lighten him up.

"I figured if you dated a jerk you'd eventually see what a catch I am," he said at last, his body softening against hers.

"Well, thanks." She crossed her own arms and pretended to huff.

"It worked, though." He drew her back, caressing her cheek before kissing her lightly on her lips.

"Are we dating?" she asked between kisses. She shifted her legs so they were in a sunny spot, folded over Scott's.

"I want something real."

This felt pretty real to her. Forever real.

"Isn't this real?"

"Very real." He kissed her again, the honey Dijon from the sandwich adding spice to their sweet, lingering kiss.

"So then?"

"Are you ready for forever?"

She tipped her head down, waiting for the tightness in her throat. It wasn't there. Sunshine radiated from her core and she smiled. Scott brought her chin back up, his eyes watchful, his body still as though he might miss the most important moment of his life if he moved a single muscle.

"I love you."

"Say it again," he breathed.

"I love you, Scott." Amber felt as though she'd just broken free of a decade's worth of chains weighing her down. She trembled with relief. She'd said it! She wanted to jump up, lean over the railing and shout out to the town that she, Amber Thompson, was in love with her best friend, Scott Malone.

"As a friend?" he asked.

"As a forever friend."

His shoulders fell before he caught himself, and she laughed.

"I'm teasing you, Officer Malone. I love you as much more than a friend." Her voice grew thick with emotion. "I can't promise you forever, but I can promise you today and tomorrow and next week. Is that enough?"

"I want you, Amber. All of you." His eyes were dark, a sign he was holding back.

"I know."

He closed them for a moment, his jaw clenching. "But I'll take whatever you can give me, as long as you give me your heart."

"It's already yours, Scott. It's already yours."

"Mom, we need to talk." Amber closed her mother's front door behind her, having completely missed catching her the day before. Gloria and Delia were sitting on the couch, bent over a magazine. "Delia, I need a moment with my mom. Actually, probably an hour. I'm sorry. I know I'm interrupting, but it's important."

"Can I wait in the other room?" Delia asked, rising from the couch cautiously. "Or…?"

"What's going on?" Gloria asked, standing in turn, her brow furrowed as she watched Delia leave the room. "You're being very rude."

"I know. I'm sorry."

"Did I do something?" Delia asked from the kitchen doorway.

"No. I'm sorry, really. I just need to talk to Mom about Dad. Aka John Abcott. Please."

Her mother paled, then sat heavily as Delia backed into the kitchen.

"We both know," Amber said.

"I should have spoken to you sooner. Both of you."

How could her mother have lived side by side with a man she

loved, in a town this small, and never told him who her daughter belonged to? Amber couldn't imagine what it must have felt like to serve him regularly in the restaurant. Or to watch him be a father to Marisa. To keep such a massive secret from him. To deny so much.

"Is he really my dad?"

Her mother nodded silently, tears sliding down the creases between her mouth and cheeks. "Oh, Amber. I'm so sorry. I'm so, so sorry. When he got divorced, I thought, *This is the time to tell him.* And then he started dating again and I didn't want to interfere. I was afraid too much time had gone by and that he would be so angry. He could have turned the whole town on me, and I was afraid it would upset you, upset your life. This town was so good for you."

Amber sat beside her mother, feeling a strange sense of calm, as she had when John had spilled his sorrows in the restaurant. It wasn't her grief. It was theirs. Their story, their battles. She'd had a good life, a good upbringing, and she couldn't imagine it being any different. If she'd known who John was earlier she might have expected things he couldn't deliver. She could easily have grown resentful toward him for not being more to her, for not giving more than he was already eking out.

"I don't want to keep this a secret, Mom. If you want me to, I'll try. But it's Blueberry Springs." By way of example, she tipped her head toward the kitchen, where, by the sound of it, her sister was washing dishes. It hadn't taken Blueberry Springs very long to see the truth about Delia. It wouldn't take them long to fit the John piece of the puzzle into place, either. Especially when Amber had been asking around and stirring things up.

"Mom?"

"Let me talk to him," she said finally. "It's time I acted my age and grew some courage, like this kid sitting next to me."

Amber laughed. "You make it sound so easy."

AMBER PASSED the rows of soccer photos lining John's law office reception area, the pictures taking on new meaning. In every single one, her father had managed to find a way to stand beside her when lining up with the team. Claiming her even though he didn't know the truth and only suspected it. He probably still didn't know the complete truth, but she hoped when her mother told him that he'd do the right thing and chase his demons away, blinding his own personal what-if alley with bright light.

Liz noticed her studying the photos. "He's quite the man, isn't he?" she said. "Always helping out in the community. His kids didn't even play soccer."

Amber ducked her head to hide any emotion that may have stolen its way to her face. "Is John available?"

"Go ahead through."

To her father's office.

"Thanks."

She felt nervous.

Her dad was a lawyer. He'd been there for her even though he hadn't been able to. He'd tried to be a good guy and not a deadbeat. He'd tried to make it work for everyone, practically straddling two lives. He'd been careful, not upsetting Gloria, but hedging his bets by watching over Amber whenever possible.

He may have made mistakes, but he'd tried to fix them to the best of his powers and abilities.

Amber peeked into his office, around the half-closed door. Not yet seeing her, he pulled off his reading glasses and pinched the bridge of his nose. Then he lifted his face to focus on the picture on the wall. Ocean. Whales.

He shook his head and replaced his glasses, diving back into the stack of papers on his desk.

Amber hesitated, unsure whether to proceed. She rapped

lightly on the door, pushing it open. "Hi. Um, do you have a minute? Liz said you're free?"

"I'm always free for you, Amber. Come in."

They stared at each other awkwardly. His possible parentage was definitely the elephant in the room and Amber was guessing her mother hadn't talked to him yet.

"What's on your mind?" He gestured to the vacant chair on the other side of his desk.

She remained standing. "I just wanted to tell you that I think Russell is dropping the whole trailer thing. So you don't need to worry about that any longer."

"Thanks. I heard. By the way, I was talking to Rosalind this morning."

"Oh? What did she have to say?" Amber hoped the woman wasn't about to kick her out with little notice, now that she wasn't sharing the place with her nephew. She'd save a lot by moving, but she'd grown fond of the old house and its quirks, and didn't have a new place lined up.

"She conveyed her apologies for her nephew's behavior and wanted me to tell you that if you're interested in still staying in her house she would reduce the rent. She wants someone there for insurance purposes while she's away. She's willing to knock the rent down by half and pay all utilities." John tugged a pink phone slip out of a stack of papers beside him, scanning it before saying, "She said with the reduction it would be five hundred a month."

"Wait. That's a 75 percent discount."

John adjusted his reading glasses. "She said the full rent was one thousand, and with the discount it would be five hundred. As well, no utility costs if you stay."

"Are you freaking kidding me?" Amber turned and stared at the ocean print. Pastel colors meant to soothe. It wasn't working. She'd financially supported Russell for the entire year he'd been writing his book. He'd not only had his paid sabbatical leave, but he'd had her covering the entire rent. He had lied, and she'd taken it like the perfect, easy target she had been, so desperate to have things work out that it had allowed her to cancel everything her brain was telling her about Russell. She had blinded herself to the truth, too afraid of what she'd see if she opened her eyes.

"Are you okay?"

"Remind me to tell you about the time I paid the entire rent while Russell Peaks wrote his novel."

John's eyebrows drew into a peak. "Did you want to take him to court?"

Amber waved away the suggestion. "If you're talking to Rosalind, tell her thanks, and that I'll stay as long as she lets me."

John made a note on the pink slip. "Have you heard from your mother?"

Amber could feel her body seizing up, trying to hide what she knew. It wasn't her secret to reveal. It was her mom's.

Don't blow it, Amber.

"I was wondering when she'll be ready." He tipped his head toward the open door, indicating that Liz was likely eavesdropping.

"Soon," Amber said, wondering how the conversation would change things for all of them. Would John claim her publicly? What would Marisa think of having a half sister?

"And how about you? How are things?" John asked. "I saw you and Scott on the water tower. He's a good man."

"Are you two together?" Liz called. "I heard you were kissing."

"Confidential conversation happening in here," John called back to her.

"Then close the door! I can hear everything the two of you are saying and it's killing me."

John grinned.

"But for the record, Amber," Liz continued, "it's about time the two of you finally got it on."

Amber glanced at her father, her face burning with embarrassment.

"Don't screw it up!" Liz added.

"I'll do my best," Amber muttered. Before she left, she quietly added, "You might want to find Gloria and make the opportunity happen. She's scared."

Even more scared than Amber was that they wouldn't claim their relationship and the child that had come out of it.

$\mathcal{A}$mber walked the sidewalks of Blueberry Springs, zigzagging her way over to Scott's. She felt excited yet apprehensive. She'd finally told him she loved him. She'd kissed him as though there was no tomorrow. But she didn't know where they went from here.

Scott had been gone all day with Jen's boyfriend, the local ranger, Rob, investigating a possible poaching incident. It was almost suppertime and she hoped Scott would be home to join her.

As she passed her mother's house, Amber paused. She'd seen John's car in the driveway earlier and it was still there. That had to be good. If they were fighting, one of them would have stormed off already. Amber mentally crossed her fingers for them and kept walking. It was never too late to find love. She only hoped they let go of the past and found whatever it was they needed for their future.

Love was a funny thing. Scott had somehow managed to hold a torch for Amber through all the years, and it looked as though her mother had done the same for John.

And while Amber wanted to believe what Scott felt was true

love, a part of her worried that those "torches" were simply optimistic dreams of what one couldn't have.

Amber's steps faltered as doubts filtered into her thoughts. She shook her head. No. She needed to stop thinking and simply allow herself to love him. Let it all hang out. He was Scott. Her best friend. The man who knew her better than she knew herself sometimes.

She was enough. Their love was enough.

With Russell it had been more about proving to the world that she could catch the attention of someone big and amazing than about her and Russell being in love. She didn't even miss him now. But Scott… Anything with him would be all-in. No hiding. He would accept nothing less than her entire heart, and would give her a level of devotion that would be both scary and so solid she could build her whole life around it.

And that was terrifying. What if he took it away? What if it wasn't as strong as they planned on it being? She would go all-in and get hurt.

Yet there was nothing she'd ever wanted so badly in her life. To go on this adventure with her best friend was the most exciting thing she could imagine doing with her coming years.

Amber knocked on Scott's door, anticipation building within her. No answer. She tried the handle. Locked. His neighbor came out onto her front step and said, "He's not home. Not that I watch. I just wanted to be able to spray my dandelions without a lecture from him on the impact of herbicides."

Amber checked her phone for text messages, knowing she didn't have any from him as he'd still be out of cell phone range.

"Did you want to leave a message for him?" the neighbor asked.

"No, it's okay. I was just coming by to say hi."

The woman gave her a knowing smile. "I think it is very cute, the two of you getting together."

"Thank you."

"I met your sister the other day, very nice woman. Very put together."

Amber pushed aside the feeling that she was being judged, and maybe coming up lacking. The two of them were different, that was all. Amber had her own value and skills. Everyone brought different talents to the table.

"Yes, I really like her," she said. "And I hope you do, too."

The neighbor paused. "Many blessings, Amber." She smiled and went back into her house.

Amber sat on Scott's steps, wondering how long it would be before he came home. He had been right. A month ago she hadn't been ready for him, and she would have messed it up with her fears and spontaneous knee-jerk reactions whenever she felt in over her head. She knew who she was now. And she'd take their relationship seriously and meet any issues head-on. She was still the person he'd always known, but she was stronger now. She could handle it, stick with it.

Amber stood. She and Scott were going to rock the whole relationship thing.

Her phone buzzed with an incoming text. It was Gloria, asking her to come over.

Was this the moment she'd been waiting for? The one where she walked into a living room to find her mother and father sharing a couch, in love, ready to be parents? Or had something gone wrong?

Bring cake, the text said.

Did her mom want to celebrate, or to stuff her feelings under layers of chocolaty frosting?

There was only one way to find out.

AMBER'S MOM held the door open as Amber awkwardly

maneuvered through the doorway with a slab cake that said *Hey, You're Pretty Great.*

"Miss me?" Amber asked, holding her cheek out for a kiss.

Her mother gave her a peck and said, "Always. What's this about?"

"I wasn't sure if I should have them put *Congratulations* or *Sorry* on it." She leaned closer and whispered, "John's car is still here."

"Nothing goes unnoticed."

"I'm allowed to stalk my own mother. So…" She passed her the cake. "What's up?"

"Amber!" John came out of the kitchen, smiling. "Let me take that," he said to Gloria. He craned his neck to reading the cake's message. "Running family joke?"

"I didn't know what to have them write on it," Amber said, feeling silly. She didn't know what was going on and was afraid to make assumptions.

"You didn't have to put anything on it," her mother stated.

"I love having them do it. Edible ink--best kind ever. And it's free."

She studied her father. He was like a blank wall, giving nothing away. Her mother seemed happy and relaxed, but Amber wasn't sure if it meant that she had told him everything or if she had decided not to.

"So what's up?" Amber asked.

"We're having a family dinner," Gloria said. She headed to the kitchen, John following her, cake in hand.

Family dinner. And John was here. Did she dare dream?

She joined them and John immediately passed her a shot of vodka. That couldn't be good, if he thought she was going to need a drink for whatever they were about to say.

"Any nuts to go with it?" she asked, feeling the need to find common ground.

"As long as they're not bar nuts," he said.

"Oh," Gloria said, rolling her eyes. "You two. The bowl of peanuts sitting on the bar at Brew Babies isn't full of fecal matter."

"Not quite accurate, Glori," John said.

Glori?

"If somebody doesn't wash their hands and then touches the nuts…"

"Why wouldn't they wash their hands?" Amber asked.

"Drunk men." John held up his palms, indicating there was nothing more that needed to be said on the subject.

"Amber, your father and I," Gloria said carefully, her chest expanding as though she'd waited her entire life to say those words, "would like your permission to tell the town about your parentage."

Father.

She was never going to get used to that.

Her mind caught up with her mother's request and Amber sat down on the nearest chair, realizing the impact that one small announcement would make.

She had a father. John was claiming her as a member of his family. She would have someone to give a Father's Day card to. There would be no more secrets in her life. Family dinners, holidays and celebrations would be more than just her and her mom. She had another half sister--Marisa. John was saying she could be a part of that. It was her choice. After all these years it came down to her.

This was huge.

"Are you sure?" she asked, watching John. His cheeks were flushed and he had one hand clapped in front of his mouth while he waited for her to reply.

"I'm sure," he said. "I am your father. I'm incredibly proud of that fact and don't want it to remain a secret any longer. I understand if you feel upset and as though you have missed out. I can't make up for what we didn't have, but I would like to be there for you in the coming years to the best of my ability. If you need me. If you want me there."

Amber was going to need another shot. She felt like bawling. To go all this time and now have him so matter-of-factly state everything she'd ever wanted.

"I'm sorry," he said stiffly. "For... for not being there."

"You've always been a significant father figure in my life."

The pinched line between John's brow eased and he visibly relaxed.

Gloria was sniffing, waving away their attention when they turned to her. "It was my fault," she said. "I denied you both your rights. And this is just... it's so much more..."

John squeezed her shoulder. "Gloria, if you had come to me several years ago I am not sure I would have been ready. I may not have embraced this to the extent that I'm willing to now. Don't blame yourself for what you did then--I'm not. I was the one who was a fool and pushed you away."

Amber's mother was crying. "No, I was the fool. I'm the one who was afraid to let you love me. It was me who felt I wasn't enough."

"And I didn't help you feel any better about it. I'm sorry." John pulled her into a hug, holding her close like a lover would. He gave her a kiss on the lips and said, "I love you, Gloria, and I have never stopped."

Amber held back tears, half wondering if she should leave the room.

"Can we make up for lost time?" John asked, and Gloria nodded.

"I would really like that," she murmured.

"So are you two a couple now?" Amber asked.

"Darned tootin'," John said.

Her mother hooked an arm around his waist. "I'm not planning on letting this man go again."

"Best words ever spoken," John said, kissing her once more.

"How do you think Marisa will feel about all of this?" Amber asked.

"I have a feeling she already suspects. She knows that I like to help you out and that Gloria was on the cruise with me."

"Yeah, about that?" Amber turned to her mother, who blushed. "Did you know he was going on the cruise?"

She nodded and John pulled her closer, smiling.

"Wait a minute. On the cruise did you two pick up where you left off twenty-five years ago?" Amber asked, recalling how happy her mom had looked getting off the plane.

"Amber, honey, you don't need to know everything."

She had gone for the man she wanted. Amber would never have believed her mom had it in her.

"Marisa and her husband are coming for supper," Gloria blurted. She checked the clock on the microwave. "In five minutes. Is that okay?"

Before Amber could answer, the doorbell chimed and her mother scurried off, John following. "They're early," he stated.

Her half sister and half brother-in-law.

The front door shut and Amber could hear Marisa say, "So are you two finally together now? 'Cause quite frankly, it's about time."

Amber watched her parents return to the room, John's arm slung around Gloria. They were smiling and in love. The parents every child hoped for, but often didn't get.

And somehow, she had finally gotten them.

"It's about time they let us in on the fact that we're half siblings, huh?" Marisa said, giving Amber a smile. She had her straight hair pulled up into a loose bun and was towing her husband, Justin Reiter, into the room. As usual, Marisa was effortlessly elegant in a linen pantsuit and looking entirely unfazed by the latest news.

"I always knew," Justin stated, arms crossed.

"You did not," Marisa said, giving him a light tap on the chest.

Amber watched the family interact. *Family.* She caught her mother's eye. It had been just the two of them for so long that to suddenly have this bounty of people in her life felt overwhelming and strangely sorrowful. She wouldn't have her mom--her first best friend--to herself any longer. Her mother was going to have all these other people to turn to, as well. John to confide in. Possibly one day soon, stepchildren with babies to dote over. A new daughter to get to know.

Amber could see herself becoming second fiddle.

The conversation buzzed around her, building and building. The easy banter, the smiles.

Something wasn't right.

It was the timing of it all. Sure, it was easy for John to say that he hadn't been ready to claim Amber earlier. She couldn't help but wonder if he was easily accepting his role now that he'd seen how Blueberry Springs had taken Delia in as one of their own. There had been no shaming of Gloria for her actions.

"How could a man like you not figure out who I was?" Amber asked her father. "Why didn't you step up? Why didn't you force the issue?"

"I didn't let him," Gloria said, her voice deathly quiet. "He tried to talk to me, to approach the subject, and I refused."

"That is the worst excuse I have ever heard for someone not pushing an issue as important as being a parent."

"You're right," John said simply, taking Amber off guard.

"We were never good enough for you," she pressed. "Why are we now?"

She knew she wasn't being particularly fair but she needed him to feel remorse for the time they'd lost as a family. She wanted him to know that the years of not having a father couldn't be erased with a few smiles and an "I'm here now." She feared that if she allowed him to act as though it was all good and wonderful that it would be like Russell all over again. She'd ignore her own feelings and allow his desires to take precedence over her own. If boundaries were going to be set, they needed to be set now.

"He was named as your legal guardian in case anything ever happened to me," her mom said.

"But not any longer?" John asked.

"She's all grown up."

He turned to Amber again. "There are a million excuses I could offer, Amber, but nothing will give you back the time you were denied. The relationship you deserved."

Her mother immediately added in his defense, "I made it pretty clear that he was not to ask me again, and I told him that you weren't his. If you're going to be mad, be mad at me."

So this was what it was like to have two parents. They stuck up for each other, but nobody stuck up for her?

"Do you like vodka?" she asked John.

He gave her a frown. "Yes."

"And actually enjoy it? Or was it all an act? Hanging out at Brew Babies all those times, eating nuts and drinking vodka?" Her voice had taken a sharp, snappy edge, her hurt showing in her voice.

Marisa gave her father a look and Amber wondered if his attempts to be in Amber's life had left his own daughter hanging. Soccer coaching. Helping Amber's friends with legal issues. Even helping her move to the city the first time, telling her he was going that way, anyway, with a trailer, to pick up something in a deal that hadn't worked out in the end. The man had told fibs in order to help her out, but how much of it was genuine and how much was guilt?

"I'm sorry if me being around took away from you--if John

trying to fix my life from the sidelines meant less father time for you," Amber said to Marisa.

"No, it was fine," she replied, looking a bit confused. "He was a great dad."

Amber, uncertain where all her sudden anger had come from, and certain she was going to say something she'd regret, quickly excused herself and flew to the washroom. She shut the door and sat on the edge of the tub, wishing there was a way she could hide out the entire night. There was just too much to process. Too overwhelming. Everyone was accepting everything, eager to be one big happy family. But what about the past? You couldn't just sweep it under the rug. There had been years of hurt and abandonment she needed to process.

Her phone buzzed with a text from Delia.

What's up?

Amber replied, *Family reunion where I'm supposed to act as though my parents' past actions haven't affected me, and be the smiling, happy kid who is delighted to have the family reunited. As you can tell, I'm having trouble finding my excitement, even though I've always wanted this.*

It was funny. Delia was the one person she felt the closest to right now. The one person who might be able to understand the mix of emotions she had swirling through her like a blizzard.

You okay?

Amber's eyes welled up and she mouthed, *No.*

It was too much. The past month had been life-changing and she was exhausted. So much had happened in so little time. So many things about her life had shifted that she didn't know what to think any longer. She didn't know what to feel. She wished she could sit on a couch eating popcorn with Delia and not think at all. Or curl up with Scott and watch some cheesy movie, with him laughing beside her. Instead, she was hiding in the bathroom on what should have been the happiest night of her life.

Amber?

Still here.

Be kind to yourself. I had a whole lifetime to get used to the idea of having another family somewhere. You only had a few weeks, and everything is changing. It's exciting, but emotionally taxing, too. You don't have to be strong. You can feel however you feel right now.

Tears blurred Delia's text message.

It's okay if it's overwhelming. It will get easier.

Promise?

Promise.

Amber loved having a big sister.

Want to play hooky? I'm babysitting Blossom in an hour, but why don't you come help me? Her parents won't mind another sitter and Blossom has the best giggle in the world. Hanging out with her puts everything into perspective. Although it doesn't seem to help the biological clock I have ticking inside me. Ha ha.

Do you have chocolate drops? Amber replied.

Three different kinds.

Amber considered the offer. She should stay here and be responsible, suck it up, act like an adult and all that annoying, exhausting business. She should do this family thing and make sure her mom knew she was okay with it. Because once it all sank in, Amber would be. But right now it was just too much load and she needed time away to process it. Gain some perspective.

Exactly what her sister was offering.

I'll be there ASAP, Amber texted back. She just hoped her mother would understand.

AMBER AND DELIA had tucked Blossom into bed, the baby drifting off to sleep with a smile on her face. Perspective for sure. Everything seemed so much more in focus and simplified when hanging out with the little girl. You had food, shelter, and love… then you had everything you needed and every reason to laugh.

Blossom's parents arrived an hour later and the sisters walked across the dewy grass to Delia's, where she unlocked the door and turned off the security alarm, Sass barking until they gave him a good ear rub.

"Where is your husband?" Amber asked.

"He's negotiating a contract in Germany at the moment. He'll be home tomorrow night."

"Do you miss him?"

"Like crazy." Delia flicked on the lights, making her way to a cabinet, where she pulled out a bag of chocolate drops, spilling the contents on the granite countertop. The spotlights above caused the wrappers to glitter like jewels, and Amber turned one over in her palm, not wanting to open it and spoil the illusion.

The two of them had been busy with the baby, taking turns tickling her tummy and making her giggle. It had been a good distraction from all that was whirling through Amber's mind, but now there was plenty of time to face it, and she was hoping her sister would turn on a movie so she could hide from the emotions.

"In your text you said your parents had reunited?" Delia asked.

"It sounds like it." Amber wasn't sure how much she should spill. She didn't want to accidentally taint her sister's view of their mother or make Delia feel as though she had to take sides. Amber also wasn't sure how much Delia wanted to play the big sister role and listen to all her woes.

"A relationship?"

Amber nodded.

"Wow. After all these years."

"I know. It's kind of sweet, but I have all this anger. He knew about me all this time and didn't do anything about it. I understand it wasn't easy, and he was trying to respect my mom's wishes while trying to help me, but at the same time…" Amber let out a shaky breath as more anger ripped through her like wildfire.

"We all want a dad who is our own personal hero. Someone who instinctively knows what we want and need, and provides it without question."

Amber nodded, blinking back tears. She focused on hooking a thumbnail under the chocolate's silver wrapper, exposing the waxy brown confection.

"I can't help but feel as though we weren't enough." Amber lowered her head into her hands. Just when she'd been feeling as though she was finally whole and didn't need a dad, this had to come along and poke holes in her bubble.

Delia unwrapped a chocolate drop, smoothing out the foil. "Do you think Blueberry Springs would have accepted the situation if your parents had come forward sooner?"

"There would have been a lot of gossip, for sure. I just--I just feel like I wasn't important enough."

Delia squeezed her hand, her own face contorted with emotion as she stood to put the kettle on for tea.

When folks in Blueberry Springs didn't like something they made it very clear. Given John's parents' disapproval of his relationship with Gloria, and his own views on babies out of wedlock--or at least given up for adoption--Amber wasn't sure how he would have reacted if Gloria had told him right away. It probably would've made life very difficult for her.

Maybe Gloria had made the right choice. Maybe both of them had, so they could have something now.

But all those years of silence. Of secrets. He'd taken the easier path--he'd remarried, instead of asking Gloria for a second chance. He'd continued his life instead of fighting to claim a daughter he believed was his.

Easy paths. Amber shook her head wryly. It wasn't as though she was in a position to judge. She'd taken the easy path with

Russell, believing him when she didn't want to, pretending to love him so she wouldn't get hurt risking it all with the man she truly loved.

However, understanding that didn't make the storm of emotions go away.

"Have I told you," Delia said, placing a cup of tea in front of Amber, "that I believe all things happen for a reason, and when they are meant to? What would have happened if this had all come out earlier?"

If John or her mother had come forward when Amber was a kid, she would undoubtedly be a different person in many ways. Which meant she might not have become the right person for Scott.

She stood suddenly, feeling as though her entire life had just dodged a bullet.

Delia looked surprised at her sudden move. "I'm sorry," her sister said. "I was just philosophizing."

"No, you're right." Amber felt as if she had to move. Had to go. Had to get back to Blueberry Springs. She was missing out on the life she was supposed to be leading--right now.

She gave her sister a massive hug. "Thank you."

"For what?"

"I wouldn't have my life any other way. Things are good. Life is good. This is where I'm supposed to be right now."

Her sister smiled, looking as though there was something else she wanted to say.

"I'm glad..." Amber began saying when her sister remained silent. She paused, trying to find the right words. "I'm glad that you and our mom have hit it off."

Delia smiled again, giving her hand a squeeze. "You're the best sister anyone could ask for, Amber." She picked up an envelope from a table in her front entry as Amber slipped on her shoes. But before she could open the front door, her sister stopped her, asking, "Is John someone you would have chosen to be your father?"

Amber would never have assumed someone like him could be her dad. He rescued girls who didn't have fathers, but she had never dared dreamed that he could really and truly be hers.

"Yes. Yes, I would choose him. Over anyone." She grinned.

"Would you choose me as a sister?" For the first time, Amber saw an inkling of uncertainty in Delia.

"Yes! Definitely, yes." Amber gave her a big hug, even though she was eager to get out of the house and off to see Scott.

"Good." Delia handed her a piece of paper, relief relaxing her features. The letterhead showed it was from the government adoption agency that had handled Delia's adoption. The same agency Amber had contacted to verify their sibling match. It looked as though Delia had contacted them as well.

Amber scanned the document and smiled. "Welcome to the family, sister."

GLORIA WAS SITTING in her car in front of Amber's house.

"What's wrong?" Amber asked, hurrying to her mom who was climbing out of the car.

"Where have you been? You weren't answering your texts. I had half the town out looking for you before Delia told me where you were."

"I'm sorry."

"I was worried. I don't want to lose you, Amber." Her mother hauled her into a hug so desperate it was like being squeezed by a python.

"You won't lose me."

"I thought this was what you wanted."

"I was just overwhelmed for a moment. I'm okay now."

Her mother let out a sigh, releasing her, but still looking so worried that Amber pulled her into another hug.

"Really. It's a lot to process, but I think it's cool that you and Dad are getting back together. And I think it's cool that he's willing to be my father and that Marisa is willing to be my sister."

Her mother's face wrinkled with pent-up emotion. "When I was younger I imagined the family I started being a lot different than this."

"You didn't imagine a daughter who loves you?"

Her mom gave her a grumpy, don't-mess-with-me look.

"You didn't imagine having a pile of kids, in-laws and a small town that felt like one big family?"

Gloria's eyes filled with tears again.

"And you didn't imagine having a man who loves you tremendously coming back to you, like the hero in some cheesy romantic flick?"

Her mother sniffled, tucking Amber's head into the crook of her neck as she pulled her into a hug.

"Who cares how you got the family," Amber continued, hugging her tightly. "The thing is that you *have* one. Two healthy daughters who get along. A man who loves you. Plus John's kids who seem willing to be a part of this crazy thing. This is family, Mom. We're lucky, you know that, right?"

"We are." Her mother had let go again and was unsuccessfully blinking back her flood of tears.

"Delia got a letter from the government, Mom. She's ours. For real."

Gloria smiled through her tears. "This *is* a bit overwhelming, isn't it?"

"One big happy family."

Her mother held her at arm's length, studying her, her mascara smeared beneath her eyes.

"Are we really okay, Amber?"

Amber knew without a doubt, right then and there, that the

buck stopped here. This was it. Her mother and her. Nothing and nobody could wedge their way between them. They had too much history to be shoehorned apart. Kind of like Amber and Scott. There was room for others to be part of their lives, but together they created an unbreakable core.

"We're going to be just fine, Mom, and so is this new family. We're going to create a new, common history. It's going to be even better than anything you could have ever imagined as a kid."

"Promise?" Gloria asked.

"Promise."

11

Amber straightened her T-shirt and ran a hand through her hair, wishing she'd opted for a jacket now that the sun was down. The air was cool and damp, Scott's front step illuminated by his porch light.

Familiar uncertainty was leeching in, undermining her courage. She'd come here to claim Scott completely. To revel in the timing of the universe, the luck of finding true love. She wanted to tell him he had her forever. Not just today, tomorrow, and next week. But forever.

The neighbor called out, "You're in luck! I saw him come home about five minutes ago."

Scott's front door opened. "Are you coming in? Or are you waiting for it to rain so you can look like a drowned rat?" He gestured to the darkening clouds bunching up behind her, collaborating to bring in a good storm.

She scurried inside as the first drops fell.

"In a hurry to see me?" he joked.

Suddenly feeling nervous and as though she had about three limbs too many, Amber stood in Scott's entry, wishing she'd done more than pop a few breath mints on her way over. Her stomach rumbled and Scott tipped his head, his eyes quiet, giving nothing away.

"Supper?" he asked at last.

"I haven't."

He checked his watch. He was wearing a well-worn waffle shirt and a pair of loose 501s that hung low on his hips. He was broad, powerful, and intoxicating.

And her best friend.

"It's after ten. Better get you fed."

He lifted his jacket off the hook. Outside, lightning flashed and thunder boomed as rain landed hard on the roof of his house.

She was supposed to come to him and prove she was ready to make their relationship more than just good intentions and conversations. She was supposed to wow him and feel as though they had made a real commitment as girlfriend and boyfriend.

And he was going out for supper. In a downpour.

"Scott."

He paused on the threshold, rain roaring behind him, the cool air wrapping around her.

"I thought maybe…" She crossed her arms, hunching against the cold spray that blew through the doorway. "Well, maybe we could talk here?"

"All I have is cereal."

"I like cereal."

Scott shut the door and hung up his coat. Wordlessly, he stepped past her, heading to his kitchen. His moves were efficient and without haste.

In the kitchen they took out cereal, bowls, spoons, and milk, saying nothing until they were seated across from each other at his small table. Scott watched her, assessing her.

"I love you, Scott."

He slowly lowered his spoon. For the first time since her arrival, the corners of his lips turned up, and his eyes sparkled as they used to whenever he saw her. In that moment she realized just how much she'd missed it, and how much she'd always counted on it. Just as she'd always counted on having her mother's undivided attention.

"What do you plan to do about it?" He leaned back in his chair, arms crossed.

Amber bit her bottom lip, shaking her head at him. He wanted to make her crawl, did he? Well, the man didn't know what he had coming.

Without breaking eye contact, she pushed her bowl to the side. Standing, she placed one knee on the table, making a quick wish that it wouldn't decide this was a great time to give up its daily battle against gravity. With her hands flat on the surface, she crawled toward Scott, pausing when her lips were a few inches from his. She allowed herself to drop her eyes and focus on his mouth, tipping her head in a way she hoped was seductive and tempting.

Scott had lined his lips up with hers, keeping them a fraction apart as he gently threaded his fingers through her locks.

She was going to kiss the stuffing out of her best friend. Her best friend who had become undeniably hot. The man of her dreams who had been there all along. Through thick and thin.

"Say it again," he whispered.

"I love you, Scott. And I'm here to make you my boyfriend. Beyond today. Beyond tomorrow or even next year. I'm yours until the end of time and nobody will ever replace you. Forever, Scott Malone."

He crushed his lips to hers, pulling her off the table and onto his lap. She wrapped her arms around his neck, savoring the way he felt strong and right in her grip. Like everything she'd always been missing.

She'd thought the biggest thing she'd wanted in her life was to know who her father was. As it turned out, what she'd actually wanted was Scott's love.

"I'll never tire hearing you saying those four words," he whispered, breaking free for a moment, before kissing her again as they let go of the last of their fears and allowed their hearts to finally unite.

"ARE you really sure you can handle forever with someone like me?" Amber asked Scott as she toyed with a tuft of chest hair. She'd seen his bare chest while swimming, but never quite like this, moving over her, and now under her as she cuddled him in a we're-officially-no-longer-just-friends glow.

Making love with Scott was like nothing she'd ever experienced. And not just because they had moved in sync, as though they'd been programmed to be together. But because she trusted him, and most of all, she trusted herself when she was with him. She wasn't worried about screwing up or what he was thinking. She'd been able to see it all on his face, feel it in the way he touched her, as though she was the most special and precious thing he'd ever had the honor of touching. She'd felt safe. There'd been no need to be bold or to try and impress him-- something she'd always felt with other lovers. She could be herself, and every single second had been special and freeing. It had felt right.

"Are you fishing for a compliment?" he asked.

Amber propped her head up so she could watch his expressions--not that he gave much away, but she could still spot a few of his tells. Right now, he felt happy, playful, safe.

"Maybe."

"For you, Amber, forever won't be long enough to show you the depth of my love."

His fingers danced up her back and she shivered, her body pushing against him for more. His arms wrapped tight around her and he took her mouth with his own. He kissed her hard and with such passion she had to cling to his shoulders to keep herself in place.

He broke away from her, their breath coming in desperate gasps.

"Will you stay?"

"The night?" she asked.

"In Blueberry Springs. For real." There was an uncertainty in his eyes she hadn't expected. A vulnerability she'd seen before, and it made her want to protect it, protect him.

"I want to stay wherever you are."

His lips curved into a grin. "That sounds good."

"As good as forever does to me."

His fingers trailed tantalizing circles on her lower back and her body responded, wanting more of him.

"Promise me something?" she asked.

"Anything."

Hmm. Anything?

"Can I drive your squad truck?"

"No."

"I had to try," she said with shrug. "Don't let my mom and dad convince us to go on double dates with them."

"Mom and Dad, huh?"

She scrunched up her nose. "It still feels really weird saying that."

"Is everything okay there? Your mom was pretty worried."

"Yeah, it's all good. Perfect, actually." Amber buried her head in the crook of his arm and groaned when she realized what she had done. She'd run. Again. Things got tough and she'd freaked out and run away from her parents instead of riding through the overwhelming feelings. "I wanted to come to you as a new Amber, but I'm still the same."

"Don't ever change."

She popped her head up, loving how she could feel his bare skin against hers. Soft and smooth, but firm, too.

"I happen to love the old Amber and don't want a new one."

"Say it again?"

"I happen to--"

"No, just the middle part."

He stared at the ceiling for a moment. "Old Amber."

She went to playfully sock him in the arm, but before she could make contact, he had her pinned under him, her wrists locked in his grip.

"That's a fun trick." She giggled.

"Wait until you see them all."

"I have plenty of time, Officer Malone."

"Have I ever told you how much it turns me on when you call me that?"

"Hmm. You may have to show me just how much. I'm having trouble getting a read on just how much it might…"

She lost her ability to think as he nuzzled her neck, his warm breath sending shivers of need through her.

"Know what else I find sexy?" he asked, laying a track of kisses across her clavicle.

"Your mom's meat loaf?"

He scowled at her. "Never. Mention my mother. In. The bedroom."

"Yeah, good idea." She could practically taste the woman's rock-hard meat loaf just thinking about it, and there were other rock-hard things she'd rather run her tongue over. "By the way, tell your mom I'm a vegetarian."

"The first time anyone sees you enjoy a hamburger at Benny's that gig's up."

"Ugh. How do you eat that stuff every week?"

"It's not about the food, Amber," he said seriously. "It's about the people. Family."

Oh. Family. Right. She had one of those now.

"Everything's going to change, isn't it?"

"It'll be good, I promise."

His hand was still exploring her curves, and she sighed against him. "Remind me why we're talking right now?"

"I was doing something important a moment ago. Now, what was it?" Scott teased, feathering her neck with light kisses.

"Tell me what else you find sexy, Officer Malone."

"You." He sucked her earlobe into his mouth, giving it a light nibble that made her breathing unsteady in all the right ways. "Believing in your own power. That emerald-green dress of yours just about undid my resolve to wait until you were ready."

"You liked the dress?"

He gave a contented moan, his hands running down her bare back. "You could dress up as slave princess Leia and still nothing would be more sexy than you owning that green dress."

"Okay, stop talking about other women in the bedroom." She grabbed the back of his neck and pulled his lips to hers. "We have a date with forever."

AMBER SCRAMBLED to tug the out-of-reach zipper into place on her green dress. Mandy and Frankie had announced three hours ago that they were getting married. Today. As in, their guests had four hours notice to get themselves into adequate shape to watch them exchange their vows in the park under the water tower. Thank goodness Amber hadn't spray painted it. It would be a little difficult to ignore the misdemeanor, with it right above the town as they watched the impromptu proclamation of undying love.

Forever.

The word had become her all-time favorite over the past few weeks.

Warm hands steadied Amber as she tried to stick a foot in a high heel while still struggling with the zipper.

"Let me," Scott said.

She relaxed, pulling her hair off her neck so Scott could help with the dress. He paused with the zipper halfway up.

"What? Is it stuck? Oh, don't tell me it's snagged. I don't have any other dresses and I'm fairly certain that Wanda's dress shop and Fran's boutique are being overrun this morning."

"I just needed a moment to take you in."

"My back?" She glanced over her shoulder at her boyfriend.

"This." His lips grazed a burning trail of heat and longing across her exposed shoulder blade, up her spine to the slope of her neck.

She shivered and turned in his arms, her lips meeting his. She would never get tired of this man. They'd been dating for two weeks and she was impatient to be with him whenever they were apart. She wanted him for the rest of time, because when they came together it was as though she not only knew herself better, but the world made more sense.

He ran his hands lightly down her arms, drawing away. "We can't be late."

His eyes promised that they would finish this after the wedding, and she reluctantly turned away so he could fasten her zipper. His fingers brushed her skin as the metallic teeth clicked together, enclosing her in the emerald outfit. She waited, expecting a light kiss on her neck, and peeked over her shoulder in question.

"We don't want to be late," he repeated, and she wasn't sure if he was talking to her or himself.

He would be worth being late for. He'd also be worth waiting for. He always was.

Once she was ready, they walked down the street, hand in hand. Amber tipped her head back, absorbing as much of the sun's heat as she could. Late spring in Blueberry Springs was a magical time and even better with a man like Scott on her arm.

"Why do you think they're suddenly getting married?" Liz asked, popping up beside them and making Amber jump.

"I think it's due time," Scott said, effectively ending the conversation with a stern look. Liz grudgingly fell back, starting the same topic with another couple joining the stream of wedding goers walking to the park.

"Oh, she's *due*," Liz said, breaking off her new conversation to pop up alongside Scott again.

"I didn't say that," he grumbled.

"It's fitting though, isn't it?" Amber asked, pointing to the water tower, where Frankie had earned his nickname Frankie-Fall-Off-The-Tower Smith back as teenagers. He'd tried to spray paint Mandy's name on the tower's side, but her scream of fear at seeing him so high up had caused him to fall. After that they hadn't dated again until recently--after Mandy had asked him to be hers by painting their names on the tower. And now here they were, getting married beneath the town's landmark.

It all fit.

Just like Amber and Scott. And maybe one day they would have their own wedding here in town, surrounded by family and friends.

Marriage. She was thinking about marriage.

Wow.

She smiled, then prodded Scott's cheek with a finger. "Smile, Mr. Serious." She could tell he was thinking about the time he'd had to bust Mandy in the midst of her proclamation--which was also an act of vandalism.

Scott obliged her with a smile, giving her a look so full of love that she tugged him against a flowering apple tree to give him a thorough kissing.

"Get a room!"

Amber turned to see Jen and Rob, grinning, holding hands.

"Hey, how are you guys?"

"The three of us are good." Jen rubbed her stomach lovingly and Amber threw out her hands.

"You're kidding!"

Jen gave a small nod.

"I knew it!" Liz exclaimed, from up ahead. "My sister owes me supper. Jen is pregnant, everyone!"

Amber hugged her friend tightly enough to lift her off the ground. The best things were happening in her life and to her friends today. Realizing she was squeezing the mom-to-be a bit too hard, she quickly released her.

"Oh, I'm so sorry. Are you okay?"

"Of course. I'm not breakable."

Rob didn't seem as certain as his girlfriend.

"So?" Amber asked Jen, falling into step behind the men, who were chatting about the town's upcoming sports day. "Are you two going to follow in Mandy's footsteps?"

"And get married?" Jen paled. "I don't know. Having a tiny baby to freak out over seems like enough for now. What about you two?"

Amber watched the men in front of them, zeroing in on Scott. She knew Jen was leery about marriage due to her own parent's messy divorce, but all Amber saw when she looked at her own parents was love. Lots of it. She turned to her friend with a mischievous shrug. "We'll see."

In her books, there was only one way to do forever.

AMBER HELD hands with Scott as Mandy and Frankie got married, Mary Alice performing the ceremony. Mandy looked amazing in her simple gown. With her blond hair smoothed into a cascade that ran down her back, and a few meadow flowers tucked in here and there, she looked like a designer-clad nymph. The sun shone on them, a gentle breeze swaying the grass and flowers behind them, the mountains a larger-than-life backdrop. It was picturesque and everything anyone would wish for a good friend's big day.

"Well, this sucks," said a voice behind her.

Amber turned to see Nicola scowling at the bride and groom.

"Why?" she whispered, aware that Scott wasn't impressed with the distraction.

"Nothing." Nicola crossed her arms, her body one big frown in the cute pencil skirt she was sporting with her new figure. "It's just so sappy," she complained. "Who needs love?"

"Apparently, you." Amber pulled Nicola away from the ceremony, gesturing to Scott that she'd be back soon and to ignore them. When they were away from the crowd, she asked, "What's wrong? What happened?"

Nicola shrugged her off, suddenly way more interested in the couple exchanging rings and looking as delighted as if they'd just been given free everything for the rest of their lives.

"What?" Amber pressed.

"*Nothing.*"

She watched Nicola trying to ignore her, then said, "Nope. Definitely something. Everybody wants to be loved. You still haven't talked to Todd, have you?"

She didn't need Nicola to reply in order to know she'd hadn't.

"Well, we can fix this," Amber declared.

"No, we can't."

"Why not tell him the truth?"

"That would be a disaster."

"And this agony isn't?"

"We're best friends."

"And?" Amber made a sweeping gesture to the two best friends who were now officially husband and wife. Not to mention her own boyfriend, who was part of her personal friends-to-lovers happily ever after.

"I broke a rule. I kissed him on Valentine's Day. He hasn't called me. We *always* talk." Nicola fidgeted with her fingers and wouldn't meet her eye.

Amber had seen Todd around Nicola last February. He'd been

possessive. Protective. He was a man in love. Amber was sure of it. "He loves you."

"Not like that."

"He hasn't called?"

Nicola shook her head forlornly.

"And have you called him?"

"No."

"Oh, geez. The two of you need to take off your scaredy-pants and get into each other's, if you know what I'm saying."

Nicola tipped her head back in surprise.

"No, really. You're unhappy. Missing him. Avoiding him. It really doesn't sound like there's much left to lose."

"Are you sure?" Nicola expression was both hopeful and terrified.

"Of course. What could be worse than this torture chamber you're currently locked in?"

Amber gave Nicola an encouraging smile as her friend wandered off, seemingly dazed, to join the line congratulating the couple.

"Were you just giving dating advice?" Jen asked, joining her.

"Yep. And it's going to work out totally awesome. People spend way too much time being afraid of putting their true emotions out there, and that's such a load of bullcrap."

"Well, now aren't you Miss Big now that you've conquered your fear of true love."

Scott joined them. "Did I hear that right? Dating advice?"

"Amber's trying to convince Nicola to run after her own happy ending. Aka Todd."

"Ah." Scott hooked an arm around Amber's waist, bringing her close enough to kiss her on the end of her nose. "Sounds like good advice."

"I thought so," she replied, going up on tiptoes to kiss him. She was glad she'd finally stopped running from her own fears and claimed what was hers--love.

Scott tugged her away from the group, murmuring things about her green dress and how it looked hugging her curves.

Amber laughed, pushing him away. "We're in public!"

"That can be remedied."

Amber caught sight of Nicola leaving the park, a new determination in her step. "Do you think she'll get the man she wants?" she murmured, gesturing toward her friend.

"That's her adventure, not ours."

Amber turned in Scott's arms, draping her arms around his neck. "And what *is* our next adventure, Officer Malone?" Now that she knew the nickname drove him wild, she was afraid she was going to wear out its effect, teasing him so she could enjoy the results.

Sure enough, he pulled her close against him, lining them up as he kissed her hard, letting the town know that she was his. A crowd cheered behind them and, smiling, Amber broke the kiss, giving the spectators a little wave.

"Did you say you know a place we can go?" she whispered.

Her mother bustled over with John, out of breath with happiness. "Did you hear the news? Jen and Rob are expecting."

"I know. Exciting, isn't it?"

John, who had his arm around Gloria's shoulders, pivoted her so his lips touched her forehead, his eyes closing in satisfaction and happiness.

He had been extra careful around Amber since her outburst at what was supposed to be their first family dinner, and she still felt bad.

"I'm glad you two are together," she told him. "That things are okay between you now."

"I'll take good care of her, Amber. You, too, if you need it."

"I know."

John watched her, then, seeming to find the answer he was looking for, gave her a short nod.

"Oh! I need to take a picture for the paper," Liz said, coming over, camera raised. "Family Reunited. I can see the caption already."

The group of them groaned.

"Where are Marisa and Justin? We need them in here, too." Liz began gesturing with her hand as though she could sweep the missing family members into the picture. She paused, looking at Scott as though trying to decide whether he should be in the photo are not.

"Scott is part of my family. He's my forever friend," Amber said, giving him a playful nudge in the ribs. He grabbed her and somehow rolled her body up his arm, slinging her over his shoulder as he carried her off.

She giggled and pretended to try and get away, secretly delighted by his behavior. How could a woman like her ever be so lucky as to have a man like him in her life? It really couldn't get much better.

Scott set her down on the walking path at the edge of the park. Guests were drifting away to join the wedding picnic in the meadow with the bride and groom. Everyone in town was dressed up, happy and content.

"Think we'll win couple of the year next time?" Amber asked, referring to Valentine's Day, when they'd won the title Greatest Couple in Blueberry Springs, but then had it taken away for not being a real couple. Next year, qualifying shouldn't be a problem.

"The only thing standing in our way was a lack of this." He leaned down, kissing her in a manner that had her arms wrapping around his neck and her body calling out to his, making short work of her concentration on everything around them.

"Glad we were able to remedy that," she said dreamily, when they came up for air.

"Me, too. I've waited too long."

"And how long have you waited, exactly?"

"Ever since you stayed in at recess and made me that valentine."

"Really?"

"It's not easy being a new kid in a town like this, especially arriving in the middle of the Valentine's Day party." He rubbed her chin with his thumb as though wiping a speck away. "I saw the real you in that moment. Someone caring and giving. Willing to put what you wanted aside to ensure someone else was okay. You're still that woman today and I still love you for it."

They kissed again, Amber's foot lifting off the ground. She forced it down again, not wanting to be a show-off, even though Scott's kisses were that amazing.

"Little kids don't love like that," she whispered.

"Well, I did. And I didn't say the type of love I had didn't change. It grew stronger, and by the time we're eighty it's going to be the strongest thing on planet earth."

"Amber Lynn Thompson." Scott got down on one knee, presenting a ring box from his pocket. "Will you marry me?"

Amber fell to her knees in front of him, her hands wrapped around his, keeping the box closed. They stared at each other for a long moment.

"Scott?"

"Yes?"

"Are you certain?"

"Yes."

"Me? Forever?" she whispered.

"A man never kids about forever."

"Even though I screw things up and say things without thinking?"

"Yes."

"And even though I have big hips and might embarrass you?"

"I happen to like your hips and find it doubtful that you could ever embarrass me."

Amber brushed away her tears, overwhelmed by Scott. His

love. His trust. His ability to see the best in her and to believe that it would always be that way, and that the two of them would only get better.

But she knew. With Scott she could be better. She *was* better. She was the Amber she was meant to be, and there was nothing better than his love. Standing there in the cool green grass, with clouds drifting over the mountain town she'd always called home, she knew at long last what it was that made this place home. And she knew that together they would always be better than the sum of their parts.

"Yes, Scott Malone. I would be more than honored to be, forever, your loving wife."

"That was even better than the yes I was hoping for."

"That's because our marriage will be extraordinary. Just like you and your love."

He slipped the ring on her finger and kissed her hand. "I love you, Amber."

"I love you, too, Officer Malone."

He swept her into his arms. "I think it's time I took you home, Mrs. Soon-To-Be-Malone."

"That sounds better than anything I could ever imagine."

"Even more than chocolate drops?" he teased.

"Definitely." She pulled his lips to hers. "There could never be anything better in the world than a best-friend fiancé."

"Or his kisses," Scott repeated, setting her down so he could kiss her thoroughly.

"Or that," she agreed when they finally broke free. They continued, hand in hand, to his house, pausing on the front step so he could unlock the door, his left hand staying on her waist as though afraid she'd disappear if they lost contact.

As he opened the door, Amber whispered, "Kiss me again, Scott. But this time, don't stop."

$* \quad * \quad *$

Thank you for reading VODKA AND CHOCOLATE DROPS. I hope you enjoyed Amber and Scott's story. What happens next in Blueberry Springs? Nicola and Todd decide whether to move past "just friends", but things get very messy for the two best friends as life and adventures mess them up. Find out how they fare and whether they get their happily ever after in TEQUILA AND CANDY DROPS.

Two best friends. One night that changes it all.

Nicola Samuels kissed the sexiest man she knows—her best friend. The man who veers away from commitment as though it's scarier than a pit of snakes. The man who, she believes, has only ever seen her as his backpacking travel buddy...

He's also the man she hasn't spoken to since The Kiss.

But Nicola's ready for the next step in life—career, marriage, family. And she knows just the man who will fit by her side—the man who makes her laugh and her heart sing. Todd Haber, her commitment-phobe BFF and the best kisser she's ever met. But can she convince him to take the next step with her?

Find TEQUILA AND CANDY DROPS in your favorite bookstore!

"I could not stop until I found out where Nicola and Todd would end up. I laughed a lot, cried a little..." —Reader review from Sheila.

SIGN UP FOR Jean's newsletter to stay in the know about deals, new books and more! www.jeanoram.com/signup

* * *

Have you fallen in love with Blueberry Springs? Catch up with your friends and their adventures in the complete Blueberry Springs series:

Book 1: Whiskey and Gumdrops (Mandy & Frankie)

Book 2: Rum and Raindrops (Jen & Rob)

Book 3: Eggnog and Candy Canes (Katie & Nash)

Book 4: Sweet Treats (3 short stories—Mandy, Amber, & Nicola)

Book 5: Vodka and Chocolate Drops (Amber & Scott)

Book 6: Tequila and Candy Drops (Nicola & Todd)

Companion Novel: Champagne and Lemon Drops (Beth & Oz)

Jean Oram is a *New York Times* and *USA Today* bestselling romance author who loves making opposites attract in tear-jerking, feel-good, sweet romances set in small towns. She grew up in a town of 100 (cats and dogs not included) and owns one pair of high heels which she has worn approximately three times in the past twenty years. Jean lives near a lake in Canada with her husband, two kids, cat, dog and those pesky deer who keep wandering into her yard to eat her rose bushes and apple trees.

Become an Official Fan: www.facebook.com/groups/jeanoramfans

Newsletter: www.jeanoram.com/signup

Twitter: www.twitter.com/jeanoram

Facebook: www.facebook.com/JeanOramAuthor

Instagram: www.instagram.com/Author_JeanOram

Website & blog: www.jeanoram.com